TO TRUST A RANCHER

DEBBI RAWLINS

MILLS & BOON

First Published in Great Britain 2018
by Mills & Boon, an imprint of HarperCollins*Publishers*
1 London Bridge Street, London, SE1 9GF

ISBN: 978-0-263-26498-2

38-0518

MIX
Paper from
responsible sources
FSC™ C007454

This book is produced from independently certified FSC™ paper to ensure responsible forest management.

For more information visit: www.harpercollins.co.uk/green

Printed and bound in Spain
by CPI, Barcelona

Debbi Rawlins grew up on the island of Oahu in Hawaii, but always loved Western movies and books. When she was twelve she spent the summer on the Big Island of Hawaii, and had the dubious honor of being thrown off her first horse. A year later, minutes before a parade started down her street, she managed to find the most skittish horse in the lineup and…you can probably guess the rest.

These days, sixty-five-plus books later, she lives on four acres in gorgeous rural Utah surrounded by dogs, cats, goats, chickens and free-range cattle who just love taking down her fence every couple years.

Also by Debbi Rawlins

Stealing the Cowboy's Heart
Her Cowboy Reunion
Alone with You
Need You Now
Behind Closed Doors
Anywhere with You
Come On Over
This Kiss
Come Closer, Cowboy
Wild for You

Chapter One

Becca Hartman's heart pounded. Today was the start of a new phase of her life. One where she'd have the time to give her son dinner and put him to bed every night, instead of just checking in on him after he was already asleep. It felt like the best gift she'd ever been given, and she didn't want to screw it up.

She checked her reflection in the bathroom mirror, trying to remember the last time she'd worn a dress. The second it hit her, she wished she hadn't tried so hard. It had been her grandfather's funeral. Two years ago. She'd rushed back to Montana but had almost missed the service. Grams had taken one look at her and cried for an hour straight.

Oh, God, Becca couldn't think about that now. She smoothed a wrinkle on the blue dress, then dabbed on some lip gloss. Satisfied that she looked presentable for the first day in her brand-new position, she went to the kitchen.

Noah sat at the table in his booster seat, making designs in his cinnamon-topped oatmeal.

"Hey, sweetie. What do you think about you and me celebrating my promotion tonight?" Becca opened the fridge and brought out the orange juice. "Pizza sound good to you?"

He was too quiet.

Reaching into the cupboard for a glass, she glanced over her shoulder. “Noah? Did you hear me?”

Making a face, he stuck the wrong side of his spoon into the cereal.

“What’s wrong? You love oatmeal.”

“I want bananas.”

“I’ll pick some up after work,” she said. “For now, you eat it like that, okay?”

From the window, she saw Isabella coming up the crumbling cement walkway, sidestepping the neighbor kid’s rusty bike. The relief that swept Becca was more proof she was far too anxious over her new job. The woman hadn’t been even a minute late in the four years she’d been watching Noah.

“Mommy?”

Becca turned a smile on him.

A glob of oatmeal hit her chin. She gasped, looked down and watched the goop slide down the front of her dress.

Noah broke into peals of laughter.

People always said the twos were terrible. Yeah, well, four was no picnic either.

Although, as a rule, Noah was a very sweet little boy. It was usually after he’d spent time with Amy that he acted out like this. She spoiled him terribly, all because she felt guilty for abandoning him. And then, consistent with their longtime friendship, Becca was left to clean up the mess.

“Noah?” She grabbed a paper towel. “Why did you do that?” She heard Isabella’s quick knock, then the door squeaked open, but Becca kept her eyes on him as she dampened the towel. “Noah? Answer me.”

He bowed his head and shrugged his thin shoulders.

Isabella quietly set her tote aside. Becca sure hoped the woman knew a trick to get the stain out, or she would have to wear the only other dress she owned. The black one, stuffed far, far back in her closet.

Her stomach rebelled at the thought.

"I'm sorry," Noah mumbled.

"You must never do that again. Do you understand?" Becca waited for his nod. "Now, aren't you going to say hello to Señora Rios?"

He looked up with a tentative smile. "*Hola*, Señora Rios."

Señora came out garbled, and Becca had to stifle a grin.

Isabella ruffled his hair. "Mmm, I smell cinnamon," she said. "Better hurry up and eat your oatmeal before I do."

Noah giggled and shoveled a big spoonful into his mouth.

"They're making you wear dresses now?" Isabella joined Becca at the sink and took the paper towel from her.

"No one said I had to." Becca gladly handed over the task before she made a mess. "I've never worked in an office before so I thought I'd go all out for my first day." She worried her lip. "Pants better be okay. I can't afford to buy new clothes."

"I bet my daughter has some things that would fit you, if you don't mind secondhand."

Becca smiled. If she did, she wouldn't have a couch or a dresser, or much of anything, really. "You don't mean Lydia…"

Nodding, Isabella used a tiny drop of dish detergent to rub out the cinnamon smudge below Becca's collarbone. "Sure I do. What's she going to do with a closet full of size sixes?"

"She'd be crazy to give up anything." Becca guessed most of it was designer stuff. "She'll lose the pregnancy weight."

"No, she won't. And now she's pregnant again."

"Well, you must be thrilled. Another grandchild for you to spoil."

Isabella snorted but couldn't help looking pleased. "There you go, good as new," she said, stepping back and inspecting her handiwork. "Don't worry if you have to stay late. Just call and I'll feed him his dinner."

"Thank you. I'll try not to be past five thirty, and I can always call Amy to come over..." Becca trailed off as she looked into Isabella's kind, knowing eyes. Amy was about as reliable as a broken watch.

"I pray for her," Isabella said, lowering her voice and glancing at Noah. "Maybe one day she'll surprise you."

Becca nodded. No prayers had helped so far, just like no amount of Becca's determination had managed to bring Amy to her senses. First, it had been Derek who'd gotten his hooks into her, and later, so had the drugs. But Isabella was a devout, churchgoing woman, and who knew, maybe her prayers carried more weight.

Noah slammed down his empty cup. "More milk."

Becca gave him a warning look. "Is that how you ask?"

"Please."

"And no more slamming your cup," Becca said, turning toward the fridge.

Isabella had already opened the door. "Go. Don't miss your bus. I'll take care of Mr. Cranky Pants," she said, the last of it loud enough for Noah to hear. It always made him laugh.

"What would I do without you?" Becca asked, giving the woman a quick hug.

"You'd do just fine." She smiled and patted Becca's cheek. "That little boy is very lucky he has you."

Becca was the lucky one, she thought as she stepped back to let Isabella pour his milk. Isabella had been a social worker and was at the hospital the day Noah was born, had been there when Amy had asked Becca to take care of him. Isabella was the only other person who knew about their complicated situation, but even she didn't know everything.

With his dark hair and blue eyes, Noah didn't resemble Amy or Derek, and sometimes it was very easy for Becca to forget that he didn't belong to her. She had no parental rights whatsoever, but Noah was hers in every other sense.

It hadn't been Amy who'd changed his first diaper or stayed up all night with him when he was sick. It had been Becca. From day one, she'd bought his crib and bottles and pretty much everything else he'd needed. Not easy on a waitress's tips. But she'd do it all over again in a heartbeat.

As for Derek, he hadn't once acknowledged the child, which was a true blessing. The guy was scum. An abuser. And every time Becca pictured her beautiful, bright-eyed friend the day she and Amy had left Montana for the neon lights of LA, Becca wanted to cry.

Amy was a mere shell of the person she used to be. Her skin was sallow, her green eyes dull and lifeless, and it seemed she could only muster a smile for Noah these days. Every time he asked Amy about the bruises and she made up a different excuse, it broke Becca's heart.

Ironic, really, that Amy had fled Blackfoot Falls to escape her abusers and then run straight into the arms of an even more sadistic man. Actually, it wasn't ironic. Becca knew better because of all the reading she'd done and the pamphlets she'd collected. It was a vicious cycle—one only Amy could break, if and when she was ready.

The knowledge didn't make Becca feel any less responsible. After all, she'd helped Amy get to LA.

She hurried to the bathroom for a tissue and to check her makeup. Getting emotional wouldn't do her any good. This promotion was a big break for her. The money, the hours, everything was finally falling into place. In a year, two tops, she hoped to have saved enough to get them out of this crappy neighborhood.

After grabbing her purse off the dresser, she stuck her head into the kitchen. Isabella was standing at the sink, humming, looking like a ray of sunshine in one of her flowery handmade dresses. Noah was still eating, his head bent over his bowl, as he intermittently hummed a few bars along with Isabella.

He looked happy.

Seeing him like that was all it took to brighten her day. She couldn't possibly love him more if he were her own child. But he wasn't, and she hoped with all her heart the day never came that she'd be forced to give him up.

Which could happen if Amy ever got clean… Though of course that was what Becca wanted for her friend. She did. Anyway, Amy would never keep them apart.

RYDER MITCHELL SAT in the dirt in the middle of the corral, waving the dust away from his face, ignoring the hooting and hollering of the three troublemakers who'd convinced him to show Toby the finer points of breaking a horse—one that was supposed to be used to a saddle.

"Hey, boss, let me give you a hand."

Ryder ignored that, too…until he heard the applause

and realized Lance was being a smartass. The other two hired men, Toby and Bear, were leaning against the corral railing with him, still laughing.

"Yeah, that's right, keep it up. Better hope some other sucker springs for your beer."

That wiped the smirks off their faces.

"Oh, come on now, we're just having some fun," Lance grumbled.

"Not all of us," Ryder muttered and pushed to his feet.

Shaking his head, Wiley snatched Ryder's dusty Stetson off the ground and handed it to him. "You ain't hurt, are you?" the foreman asked in a quiet voice.

Ryder shook his head. "Just my pride."

"Sure you didn't break your check-writing hand with that stupid stunt?" Wiley asked, loud enough for the horses in the pasture to hear him.

Wiley ignored the kid as he glanced toward the house. "Does Gail have their paychecks? I can go get them from her. Unless they're still in your office."

The bunkhouse door slammed, giving Ryder a few moments to think it over. Otis, who did the cooking for the men, hobbled outside, using his arm to block the late-afternoon sun as he joined the other men at the railing.

Ryder looked back at Wiley. The poor guy had developed a thing for Ryder's mother. Gail didn't have a clue, and he doubted Wiley would ever act on his feelings. The man had been a friend to Ryder's father until he'd died three years ago, and Wiley had started working for the family long before that.

In his mid-fifties now, he had some gray at his temples and in his sideburns. But he was as lean and muscled as any of the younger men who worked under him. He was also honest and hardworking. Gail could do a lot worse… once she finished grieving. It sure would help if his flaky sister called more often. Better yet, Amy needed to pay their mom a damn visit once in a while.

It was coming up on Thanksgiving—maybe she'd surprise them. Yeah, he wouldn't take a dollar bet on that happening.

"I'm not sure where I left the payroll," Ryder said finally. "If you don't mind, check with her."

"No problem." Wiley took off his hat and ran a hand through his hair as he headed toward the house.

The truth was, Ryder didn't know how he'd feel if the two of them ever got together. He wanted to see his mom happy again, though. And if Wiley could bring a sparkle back to her eyes, well, who was Ryder to judge?

Hell, he had no business having an opinion, period. He hadn't been able to make his own marriage work. Clearly, he was better at ranching.

He looked around, filled with a bone-deep sense of satisfaction. The main barn had been completely overhauled, and next, he planned to reinforce and repaint the barn behind the stable, which now had a new roof. As did both the calving and equipment sheds.

Over the winter, they'd have to move the north fence line since he'd just bought another seven hundred acres from Alvin Medina. By staying focused and investing well, Ryder had the cash to get a good deal. And he still had enough money to do more remodeling in the house.

So far, he'd made the kitchen and family room easier to navigate now that his mom used a cane and sometimes a walker. She'd always enjoyed cooking, up until the day his dad had passed. Since then, she'd lost interest in most of her hobbies. But now, with all her new, high-end appliances, she'd been trying out different recipes like she used to.

"You were joking about the beer, right, boss?" Toby

said, pushing his long hair out of his eyes. "It's a tradition. You buy us a case every Friday."

"So now you expect it?"

"Well, yeah."

Ryder just shook his head. "I think Wiley put it in the barn fridge."

Toby grinned. "Sweet."

Watching him walk toward his pal, Bear, something occurred to Ryder. "Hey, Toby."

He stopped, turned. "Yeah, boss?"

"How old are you?"

Looking sheepish, Toby hesitated. "I'm not leaving the property. Just playing cards in the bunkhouse tonight."

Ryder sighed. "How old?"

"Almost twenty-one."

Almost.

Well, hell. Basically, he'd been buying beer for a minor. He wondered if Wiley knew. With Ryder away on business so much, Wiley had a better handle on what was going on. "What about Bear?"

"Oh, he's twenty-three."

Ryder slapped the Stetson against his thigh, sending up a cloud of dust. "Look, even if you have only one beer, you and your truck don't leave the property. Got it?"

"I swear I won't, and my birthday's in six weeks, so I'll be all legal and everything."

Nodding, Ryder headed toward his office. Not that he'd admit it, but he'd been drinking beer since he was eighteen. Just on weekends, along with his college roommates. None of them had been the type to get too drunk or do anything crazy. It had been a rite of passage, a part of the college experience and nothing more.

It puzzled him that he'd suddenly thought to ask. Toby had been working for them for about five months. And at over six feet, with a husky build, he could easily pass for mid-twenties.

Ryder was the problem. Some of the newer hires were beginning to look young because he felt old. Arguably, at thirty-two, he should be in his prime. But in the ten years since graduating from college, he'd been married, divorced, lost contact with his only sister, buried his father, had been consoling his mother and had nearly doubled the size of the family ranch. So yeah, he felt like he'd already lived two lifetimes.

He heard the front door and glanced toward the porch. His mom had walked out with Wiley. Wrapped in a coat that was too warm for the relatively mild November air and leaning on her cane, she waved at Ryder. Wiley stood beside her, looking uncertain and helpless.

Ryder understood completely.

Maybe he was wrong about the attraction. Maybe Wiley was just plain worried about her like Ryder was. They hadn't talked about it, but Gail hadn't been the same since his dad's death, and anyone who knew her would have to be blind not to see how much she'd aged.

As if the tragedy hadn't been enough, one of their neighbors had been taken by cancer a short time later. Shirley Hancock and his mom hadn't been particularly close, but the woman's granddaughter, Becca, was the little hellion who'd dragged Amy off to LA with her. Though as it turned out, Becca had been much better about keeping in touch with her grandparents, who'd shared everything with the Mitchells. But after they'd passed, news of Amy had dried up.

Ryder stopped midstride and redirected his steps toward the house. Toward his mom.

He didn't know why he hadn't thought of it before, probably because he'd been too damn focused on expanding the ranch and doubling profits. But maybe it was time for him to take a little personal trip.

And drag his selfish baby sister back by the scruff of her neck.

Chapter Two

Becca had just sat down—no, collapsed was a better description—when she heard the doorbell. Waitressing wasn't an easy job. But who knew being confined to an office all day trying to familiarize herself with a bunch of different terms would drain the life out of her? And it was only day three.

It took some effort to get off the chair, and then she heard the patter of little feet rushing to the door. "Noah, do not open—"

"Aunt Amy!"

Becca sighed. Well, at least it wasn't an ax murderer, but Noah knew better.

"How's my little man?"

Becca came from the kitchen just as Amy scooped him up in her arms and swung him around.

"Ouch!"

His shoe had hit the doorframe.

"What happened?" Amy asked, her eyes wide and surprisingly clear.

"Come in so I can close the door." Becca noticed the kid from two houses down loitering on the sidewalk with his scary friends, trying to get a look inside. She probably should let him see. He'd find out real quick there was nothing worth stealing.

"You're getting heavy, kiddo," Amy said as she set Noah down. Then she turned a quizzical look at Becca. "I stopped at the restaurant. They said you're not there anymore."

"No, but I still work for Warren. He promoted me to an office job."

"Wow, look at you." Amy grinned. "I always knew you'd end up some big shot."

Becca laughed. "Yeah, that won't be happening anytime soon."

"What's that?" Noah asked, tugging on Amy's T-shirt and pointing to the bag she was holding.

She raised her eyebrows at him. "Your mommy was talking. Don't interrupt her."

Noah stuck out his bottom lip and pouted.

Becca was shocked. She was pretty sure this was the first time Amy had ever corrected him. For anything. As for referring to Becca as Mommy, that had been the first recognizable word he'd uttered, directed at Becca. They'd agreed it was for the best, certainly less confusing for him. But she sometimes worried that it hurt Amy's feelings.

"How about some lemonade, you two?"

After briefly hesitating, Amy said, "Sure. I have time for a glass." Her hair looked freshly washed, and was pulled back in a neat ponytail. Even her face had cleared up a bit. A small thing but still progress.

On her way to the kitchen, Becca smiled when she heard Noah ask about the bag again. She brought the pitcher of lemonade out of the fridge, her gaze catching on the veggies she'd been cutting up at the table. "Hey, Amy, can you stay for dinner?"

"Nope. Sorry."

Becca would've been surprised if she'd agreed. Derek

kept her on a short leash, which made her visits infrequent and brief. Next week was Thanksgiving. Even though Becca knew the calls home had dwindled, she would remind Amy while she seemed clearheaded.

Noah let out a whoop.

A toy, of course.

Becca hoped it was age appropriate so she wouldn't have to be the bad guy. Again.

She carried the glasses and Noah's plastic cup into the tiny living room. The torn bag was on the floor next to him. Amy was perched at the edge of the couch, holding two plain white envelopes as she watched Noah tear into the package.

"Don't worry," she said, taking her lemonade. "It's a Lego truck. Age three and up."

"Perfect." Becca returned her smile. "Noah? I'm putting your cup right here." She set it on the corner of the end table. "Look up, please."

Grudgingly, he did.

"Do you see it?"

"Yes, Mommy. Thank you."

"You're welcome. Be careful you don't spill it." She sat next to Amy and watched him, noting his frustration at being unable to open the box quickly enough. She didn't want it escalating into a tantrum.

"You're so good with him," Amy said softly, her gaze as wistful as her sigh.

"So are you. He loves it when you visit, or take him for an outing."

"Yeah, but you're here day in and day out. Plus work a full-time job. How do you have the patience?"

Becca smiled. "I wouldn't trade it for anything. Seriously," she added when Amy looked doubtful. "I still have faith you'll get it together and leave you-know-who."

They were speaking softly, but Becca glanced over to make sure Noah wasn't listening. "My new job pays a lot more, and I'm hoping to find a bigger place. You'll be able to move in with us."

Amy sniffled, not from a cold or allergies—it was the drugs. "Wouldn't that be something?"

"It's going to happen. You'll see."

"Sometimes your optimism really annoys the sh—crap out of me."

"I know," Becca said, laughing.

Amy smiled.

"Wow!" Noah freed the truck from its box and held it up high as he jumped up and down. "Neato."

"Wow is right," Becca said. "Did you thank your—" The word got stuck in her mouth.

"Yes," Amy said, "he was very good and remembered to thank his aunt Amy."

They didn't speak for a while but watched Noah play with his toy and fill the silence with *vroom* sounds as he rolled the truck around.

"What time is it?" Amy asked suddenly.

Becca patted her pocket. Her phone was in the kitchen. "About six thirty, I think."

Amy cursed under her breath. "I wish I could stay longer, but I don't need Derek getting pissed off or paranoid." She glanced at the envelopes in her hand, then looked at Noah. "I'm gonna do it," she said in a quiet voice. "I'm gonna leave him."

Not sure she'd heard correctly over Noah's excitement, Becca leaned closer to Amy. "Derek?" she whispered. "You're—"

Amy nodded. "I've stashed some money. It's not much," she said, pushing one of the envelopes at Becca, who refused it. "But it should help a little—"

"Wait. When?"

"Soon."

"Soon? Come on, Amy. You can't just—"

"Please, just listen. It's important." Amy's voice shook. Her gaze darted to Noah, who was happily playing with his new toy and paying them no mind. "Derek's going to meet someone at the border next week. I don't know when for sure."

"You'll come here, right? He doesn't know where I live."

"I'm not coming anywhere near you or Noah. Not for a while." Amy swallowed. "He's dangerous, Bec."

"I know."

"No." Amy's eyes closed briefly. "You don't."

Becca bit her lip. Every part of her wanted to hang on to her friend so tight she couldn't go back to that monster. When Becca had first met Derek, he'd been all dimples and charm. She'd seen him twice after that and thought something was off about him. But not Amy. She'd fallen hard and fast.

"Where will you go?"

"I don't know yet. But I'll call you. Take the money, Bec."

"Okay, now you listen, because you aren't thinking clearly. You're going to need cash, a lot of it. First thing you should do is buy a phone he can't track. They sell cheap ones, no contract. You don't have to give your name or anything." Becca's mouth was so dry she had to stop and take a quick sip of lemonade. Damn, she wished she had more cash in the house. "What about a women's shelter? You'd be safe. Even if he knew you were there, he couldn't get to you—"

"Becca?"

"I still have some pamphlets." She started to rise, but Amy caught her arm.

"Becca, I'll be fine."

"But you don't even know where you're going. You haven't thought this through."

"No, I haven't, but only because I just found out he'll be gone. Without dragging me along with him. That almost never happens. I can't blow this shot."

"You know the Mexican border is only four hours away. He might not be gone very long."

"A deal went sideways, and he's in deep shit over it." A nasty smile lifted her lips. "He's gotta make things right, whatever it takes."

"So let's make a plan. Right now. We can figure it out."

Amy shook her head. "If I'm away too long, he'll get suspicious," she said, sniffling again and making Becca wonder if it was the next fix that had her anxious to leave. "I have money, okay? So don't worry about that." She inhaled deeply. "There is something you can do for me, though."

"Name it."

"If you don't hear from me in a week, I'd like you to take Noah home, to Blackfoot Falls. To my family. *His* family. Let my mom raise him, out in the country where he'll be safe and happy. Derek still doesn't know anything about where we came from."

Shock spread through every part of Becca's body. Her mouth opened, but she couldn't seem to make her jaw work.

"I know you're surprised," Amy said quietly.

"Surprised? Are you forgetting why we left in the first place?"

Amy slowly shook her head, her eyes filling with

tears. "You can have your life back, Bec. I bet you haven't had a date in five years."

"You think I care about that?" Becca hadn't meant to raise her voice. Thank God Noah was still occupied. "How can you ask me to put him in that—that environment?"

Amy dropped both envelopes on the couch. "If you don't hear from me in a week, open the second envelope."

Becca stared at it, her insides clenching. When she looked up, her friend looked away. "Amy, you're scaring me. Let me help you."

"It's just a letter, but it'll explain a lot. Just promise me you'll wait the week."

"Watch this…" Noah lifted the truck, pretending it was an airplane.

Amy turned and smiled at him. A tear slipped down her cheek and she dashed it away.

"Mommy, look."

Becca managed a smile, and her "look at you," sounded somewhat natural despite the fear churning in her stomach. "Don't go back, Amy," she pleaded, lowering her voice. "You've already made the decision. Just stay. I have clothes for you, anything you need…"

Amy stood. "If I wait till he's gone, I'll have a head start. God, I hope he doesn't remember you worked at the restaurant. Don't underestimate Derek—he might come looking for him," she said, staring fearfully at Noah.

"Why?"

"For leverage. Hell, for just about anything, if it means saving his own ass."

The air fled Becca's lungs. "I'm begging you, Amy. Let me help you."

"Remember, wait a week." Amy took a step and stopped, her moist eyes dark with misery. "Please don't hate me," she whispered, then picked up Noah and hugged him so tight he whimpered. "Bye, little man. I love you with all my heart."

"Amy, wait."

"I love you, too, Becca," she said, and was out the door before Becca could take another breath.

BECCA STOOD AT her bedroom window, staring out into the gathering darkness. A gang of rough-looking neighborhood kids huddled at the corner, oblivious to the police cruiser that had circled for the third time.

Six days, and not a word from Amy. Becca was a complete wreck. She tried to remember how they'd left it, exactly, but she'd been too rattled. Shouldn't Amy have called by now? Just to let Becca know she'd gotten away from Derek. A few seconds. That's all it would've taken.

Unless she couldn't because the bastard had caught her.

Becca shuddered at the thought.

Trying to concentrate at work took all her energy. Hard to learn anything new with the attention span of a two-year-old. Her mind kept spiraling to dark places and robbing her of hope.

Her gaze strayed to the envelope she'd stupidly left in full view on the dresser. Every time she saw it her anxiety level rose. Twice now, she'd almost given in to curiosity. But, no, she hadn't read the letter.

She had checked the envelope with the money, though. Not a huge amount, but more than she'd expected. Which bothered her. A lot. If Amy had truly thought she could escape, she would've known she needed every penny.

Becca briefly closed her eyes. Why had she let Amy leave? If she'd had just a little more time to convince her…

Noah stirred. Curled up on her bed, sound asleep, he wrapped one small arm around the pillow. It was seven thirty. If she didn't wake him soon, tomorrow morning he'd be springing out of bed before the rooster crowed.

The thought surprised her. The saying had been one of her grandmother's favorites. Even as the memory made Becca smile, it saddened her. She missed both her grandparents, but she'd been especially close to Grams. No kinder, more generous woman had ever walked the earth. Always ready to listen, never judging. Oh, how Becca would've loved her advice right about now.

Her cell rang, startling her. It wasn't Amy, though.

Maureen managed the downtown restaurant where Becca used to work. The busy dinner hour was an odd time to call. "Hey, Maureen, what's up?"

"Listen, I only have a minute and it's probably nothing, but I thought you should know. Some creepy-looking dude was in here asking for you. Long hair, lots of tats, rides a Harley. Didn't give his name."

Becca's heart nearly stopped. "How long ago?"

"Thirty minutes, maybe? We're swamped or I would've called sooner."

"No, that's fine. I appreciate the heads-up." Her voice sounded remarkably calm considering she could barely breathe. "What did you tell him?"

"Just that you didn't work here anymore and I didn't know where you were. I hope that was okay."

"Perfect. Thank you." She knew Maureen was curious, but the restaurant was busy and Becca easily ended the call.

She pressed a hand to her roiling stomach. Did this mean Amy had gotten away and he was looking for her? He would assume Becca knew her whereabouts. But if

Amy had escaped, wouldn't she have called? She knew Becca was worried…

In a few steps, she had the envelope in her trembling hand. She glanced at Noah, still asleep, before she tore through the flap.

The letter was short, written in Amy's scratchy handwriting. Moving to the doorway where the light was better, Becca started to read.

Her stomach lurched with each sentence, and she finished in a stupor.

She blinked, but the haze wouldn't clear.

Amy had lied. About her father, her brother, the abuse. About everything. And she'd used those lies to get Becca to come with her to LA.

Anger overwhelmed every other emotion spinning uncontrollably inside her. Becca hadn't wanted to leave. She'd enrolled in community college, paid for it herself with her savings. She'd found a part-time job that had accommodated her school schedule, and best of all, she could've done it all while staying with her grandparents.

A sob slipped past her lips and she quickly covered her mouth.

Oh, God, how she'd hurt them, the two people who'd loved her more than anything else in the world. Who would've moved mountains for her. And she'd done it all for nothing.

The disappointment in Grams's eyes the day Becca had left still haunted her. It would always haunt her. All because Amy had lied out of complete and utter selfishness. And her dad and brother? The hatred that had burned in Becca's gut when she'd thought Ryder had—

Another sob threatened. She turned away from the bedroom at the same time her cell rang. Noah lifted his head, rubbing his eyes.

She didn't recognize the caller's number. Maybe the burner phone she'd suggested to Amy?

Becca answered quickly.

"You have something that belongs to me, bitch." Derek's menacing voice came through loud and clear. "And I want him back."

Chapter Three

Blackfoot Falls had changed in the years since Becca had last been home. Lots of shops that had closed because of the poor economy were now open again, as well as new stores she didn't recognize.

Someone had bought the old boardinghouse on the south side of town and turned it into a cute inn that kept the early-1900s feel intact. It would've been fun to stay there, but the new motel on the opposite end of town had larger rooms and was ten dollars cheaper. Since Becca had no idea how long they would be away, she needed to watch every penny.

After Derek's call, she'd known she had to get out of town, and coming home was the most sensible option. Noah's safety was her first concern while she waited for Amy to call. But if Amy didn't, and that was a real possibility no matter how much Becca hoped otherwise, she needed a clear head to tackle the gut-wrenching decision that would change her and Noah's life forever.

So she'd called her boss and pleaded for some personal leave due to a family emergency, which wasn't a lie at all. She'd worried, though, about where they'd stay until she found out what was going on with her grandparents' house. It was old to begin with, and being vacant for so long could mean it wasn't move-in ready.

Becca was happy with her choice. Their second-floor room was clean and comfortable, the queen-size bed had a mauve and green comforter that matched the curtains. A small round table with two sturdy chairs stood near a window facing the Rockies. She hadn't realized just how much she'd missed the mountains, and a sky that was actually blue.

It took her two trips to bring up their gear, three bags of ice and the cooler she'd packed with Noah's snacks and drinks. Next on the list was a run to the Food Mart. After driving for sixteen hours, all she wanted was to curl up and sleep for a week. But they needed some reasonably healthy food they could eat in the room. Restaurant meals weren't in her budget.

"Mommy, I'm hungry," Noah said, almost on cue as they stepped out into the corridor.

"I know, sweetie. We're going to the store right now." She pulled the door closed and tested the knob to make sure the lock had engaged.

"I'm hungry *now*," he whined and took her hand.

"Would you like an apple?"

He made a face.

Becca smiled, knowing he was hoping for a cookie. "Guess you're not that hungry then, huh?"

He started to pout, then saw the elevator. "Mommy, let's ride that again." His hand slipped out of hers and he raced ahead. "I'll push the button."

"Wait. You don't know which—" Sighing, she caught up to him just as the doors slid open. Oh, well, they'd ride up first. She held onto his arm. "Noah, don't touch the button until I tell you. And no more running inside. You know better."

His sulkiness didn't last long. He was too excited about their *big 'venture*. Becca had encouraged the idea to keep his spirits up. Sometimes, when her mind started wandering to bad places, she needed the illusion herself.

The grocery store was only a five-minute walk but she took the car. Inevitably she'd be running into people she knew, and there would be questions. Many, many questions. But she wasn't prepared to be an open target yet.

She thought again about Amy's family and the decision that had to be made. Becca felt sick every time she remembered the vile thoughts she'd harbored toward the Mitchells. As if that wasn't bad enough, she sometimes wished she'd discover that Amy hadn't lied back then and that her letter was the lie. Maybe now that her father had passed and Ryder was married, she'd felt it was all right to bring Noah to her mother.

No, that was panic talking. Becca didn't want the lies she'd believed to be true at all.

She sighed. This trip would tell her a lot. She just hoped she was strong enough to make the hardest decision of her life.

RYDER TURNED INTO the parking lot of the Food Mart, not at all surprised that it was jam-packed. He'd tried to warn his mom. With Thanksgiving in three days, naturally the place would be a zoo. Why so many people waited until the last minute was one of life's eternal mysteries.

"There's a spot," she said, pointing. "Three down from the entrance. It's a good thing we brought my car. Your truck never could've squeezed in."

Ryder didn't comment. He hated driving the compact. It was too uncomfortable for someone over six feet, but since her stroke, he knew getting in and out of the car was easier on her. Since she didn't drive anymore, he'd considered trading it in for a medium-size sedan. But she loved the old Ford, and even after two years, her doctor insisted that a great deal of her problems were psychosomatic.

The prognosis had nearly earned poor old Doc Heaton a whack from his patient's cane. She'd even used a couple of words Ryder was surprised she knew. He and the doc didn't talk about it anymore…at least not in her presence.

On occasion, Ryder suggested she try setting the cane aside for an hour, just to see how she fared. She always looked so hurt that her only son didn't believe her.

After he helped her out of the car, he brought her a shopping cart so she could lean on it instead of the cane.

In truth, she didn't have to do any of the shopping. Otis came into town once a week to keep the bunkhouse well-stocked. He always offered to take her list with him. But Ryder knew this was more a social outing for her, so even though he'd rather have a tooth pulled, every week when he wasn't away on business, he brought her to town.

Sometimes they'd go home with only a head of lettuce and a bag of carrots. Since he hadn't provided her with a single grandchild before he and Leanne had divorced, he figured the penance could've been a lot worse.

While she ambled down each aisle, stopping every few minutes to talk, he headed over to the deli case. The ready-made food choices had expanded. Marvin, the owner, was stepping up his game.

"Are you sure you're only four? You eat like a horse." The woman's voice sounded vaguely familiar. Ryder turned toward it.

"I'm not a horse. I'm a boy." The kid was grinning and tugging on the woman's hand.

She had her back to Ryder, her wavy brown hair spilling down just past her shoulders. Average height. Slim build. Wearing jeans and a sweater like most of the shoppers. Being a regular now, thanks to his mom, he'd gotten to know more people in the past two years than he had throughout most of his youth. But he didn't know her.

Laughing, she grabbed a bag of chips off the shelf and dropped it into her cart.

Ryder still couldn't get a look at her face.

"Oh, my word, I haven't seen you in years." Millie Perkins stopped her cart seconds from colliding with the mystery woman. "Becca, right? Becca Hartman?"

Ryder's chest constricted. Becca? Here in Blackfoot Falls? Was Amy here, too?

"Nice to see you, Mrs. Perkins. How are you?"

"Oh, can't complain. Wouldn't do any good if I did, now would it? How's your mom? Is she still living up in Alaska?"

"She sure is."

"You have such an adorable little boy." Millie smiled at him. "What's your name, sweet pea?"

"I'm not a pea," he said, scrunching up his face. "I'm a boy."

Becca gasped. "Noah. Mind your manners."

"Oh, he's fine." Millie bent to ruffle his hair.

Ryder grabbed a box of crackers and pretended to read the label, while he listened and studied Becca. Last time he'd seen her, she'd been eighteen and as thin as a fence post. He'd just married Leanne and they'd been working on plans for their new home when Becca had convinced Amy to run off with her.

His sister had sworn up and down she'd be back in a year, two tops. The plan had been to help Becca get settled, then come back to attend college an hour away. After Amy had missed three Christmases in a row, it was clear to Ryder that she'd made a new life for herself. And she wasn't coming back. His parents had refused to believe it.

Ryder wished she'd had the decency to be straight with

them. Whoever had coined the phrase *blood is thicker than water* had come up short.

"So are you here for good?" Millie asked.

That got Ryder's attention again.

Becca shook her head. "Just visiting."

"What about your friend? You know, Gail Mitchell's girl," Millie said. "Amy? Is she here with you?"

The stricken look on Becca's face caught Ryder off guard. Her posture changed. She reached for her son's hand. And when she finally smiled, he saw a slight quiver, and he knew in his soul that something had happened to Amy.

"No," Becca said calmly. "Amy couldn't make it."

"Ouch." The kid scowled at her. "You're squeezing too hard."

"I'm sorry, sweetie. I bet you're hungry."

He nodded vigorously.

"Let's see what we can do about that." Becca looked at Millie. "It was nice seeing you, Mrs. Perkins. Please give my best to Mr. Perkins."

"Well, maybe we can have a cup of tea and a nice chat before you leave." Millie glanced at the contents of Becca's cart. "Looks like you'll be here awhile."

Becca laughed. "Have you forgotten how much a four-year-old can put away?" she said, already steering the cart and the boy around Millie.

"Oh, heavens, yes. I remember."

Ryder did a quick mental calculation. The boy would've been two years old by the time Becca's grandmother had died. As far as he knew, Shirley hadn't mentioned anything about Becca having a kid. When it came to news from LA, his mom never skipped a word.

As soon as she made it past Millie, Ryder put the crackers back on the shelf. Time to see what Becca had to say about Amy to his face. He sidestepped the boxed stuffing display so he could cut her off, then remembered his mom. Dammit. He needed to get to Becca first.

He circled around the refrigerator case and stepped in front of her cart.

Eyes widening, she gasped. "Ryder."

"Hello, Becca."

"Hi." Her gaze darted briefly to the boy. "This is a surprise."

"That's an understatement."

"Right." She cleared her throat. "I planned on calling you and your mom later."

He raised his eyebrows.

"You know, after we settled in. We just got to town an hour ago."

Okay, maybe she was telling the truth and she had intended to get in touch. But why look so nervous? "Where's Amy?" he asked, holding Becca's gaze.

She shook her head. Sadness flickered in her hazel eyes before she blinked and looked away. "I think she had other plans for the—" She pressed her lips together and swallowed.

"What? For Thanksgiving? Let's see, that makes seven of them that she's missed now?"

"I'm not her keeper," Becca said, her voice barely a whisper. "Amy does what she wants."

"Aunt Amy gave me a neato truck." The kid grinned up at him. "You wanna see it?"

"Noah." Becca tugged at his hand. "It's not here."

"It's in the car."

"No, it's not…"

Ryder felt a surge of relief. He didn't know what had given him the sick feeling that something had happened to his sister. If that were true, she wouldn't be buying the kid toys. "Hey, sport, when did your aunt buy you the truck?"

"Sport?" The boy wrinkled his nose. "My name is Noah."

"Ah." Ryder knew Becca was watching them closely, and something sure was making her jumpy. What the hell did she think he was going to do to her kid? "Sorry. Noah."

"What's your name?"

"Ryder." He stuck his hand out. "Pleased to meet you, Noah."

The little guy just frowned at his hand at first, then looked at Becca.

She smiled at him. "It's okay, sweetie," she said, brushing the hair out of his eyes. "Ryder just wants to shake your hand."

His mouth formed an "oh" but without the sound, then he slapped his palm against Ryder's and started giggling.

In spite of himself, Ryder smiled. Whatever was up with Amy wasn't the kid's fault. "That's quite a grip you've got there," he said as his hand swallowed Noah's.

"Becca! Oh, my goodness!"

At the sound of his mom's voice, Ryder flinched. Why now? Dammit.

Becca jumped.

He turned and watched his mom, gripping the cart with one hand and her cane with the other, hurrying toward them.

"Hello, Mrs. Mitchell." Becca's gaze flew to the cane.

She looked as if she didn't know how she should greet his mom, which really pissed him off. Becca had spent most of her teens at their ranch, eaten a lot of dinners with the family. He was seven years older than Amy and hadn't paid much attention to her and her friends, but he remembered that Becca loved horses. Always wanted to hang around the stables. She'd been close to her grandparents, but the Hancocks weren't ranchers.

Becca finally stepped forward and embraced his mom in an earnest hug. When she moved back, he saw the tears in her eyes before she blinked them away.

The relief he'd felt over Amy disappeared. Something was wrong. And damned if he wouldn't wring every last detail out of her.

Chapter Four

Becca shouldn't have been surprised to run into Amy's mom and brother. Less than twenty-five hundred people lived in the county and half of them ended up in town for one reason or another most days.

"So when did you arrive?" Mrs. Mitchell asked, her hopeful gaze sweeping the area. "Amy didn't mention you all were coming. She's here with you, isn't she?"

Becca felt terrible over the woman's attempt to sound casual when she was anything but. She swallowed and made the mistake of glancing at Ryder. The contempt in his eyes startled her. While he hadn't jumped for joy over seeing her, he'd been okay a few moments ago.

She refocused on Mrs. Mitchell. "No, I'm sorry," Becca said, saddened by the woman's obvious disappointment. A mother never gave up hope. Becca understood that now. "Amy wanted to come, but the trip was a last-minute decision on my part and she already had plans." Becca paused. "She sends her love, though."

The ensuing silence couldn't have been more awkward. Becca wanted to disappear. Gail Mitchell had always been so kind to her. Becca could've tried to sound more convincing.

Mrs. Mitchell gave her a resigned smile. "Well, I'm very glad to see you, Becca. You look all grown-up, and so pretty," she said with a brief glance at her son. "Isn't she pretty, Ryder?"

Heat stung Becca's cheeks. She tried not to look at him. He hadn't responded, which was more than okay with her. Except then she had to look, couldn't stop herself.

He hadn't changed all that much in the seven years. His chest and shoulders looked a bit broader, but then ranching tended to breed muscular men. His sandy-brown hair was longer now, waving just above his shirt collar very much like—

Stricken by a sudden realization, she jerked her gaze up and met Ryder's dark blue eyes.

Why hadn't she seen the resemblance before?

"Mommy?" Noah frowned up at her. "Mommy, what's wrong?"

She held back a sigh. "Nothing, sweetie," she said, giving him a smile.

Gail blinked at him, as if seeing him for the first time. "And who is this adorable young man?" She bent down to Noah's level, and Ryder was instantly at her side, holding on to her arm while she leaned heavily on the cane.

Becca's gaze went straight to the stubborn wave in his hair in the exact spot and angle as Noah's.

At one point in her teens, she could've described Ryder down to the very last detail. She'd been such a pathetic cliché, crushing on her best friend's older brother. "Noah, this is Mrs. Mitchell. Answer her, please."

"I'm Noah." He grinned big. "You wanna see my truck?"

Mrs. Mitchell laughed. Even Ryder smiled.

"Of course I do. Where is it?" She pretended to look around for it. "Is it in your pocket?"

"No." Gurgling with laughter, he leaned into Becca. "It's too big."

Mrs. Mitchell beamed at him, her glow of delight taking years off her face. How had she aged so much since the last time Becca had been home? Her short dark hair had streaks of gray and there were new lines on her face that Becca doubted were from laughter. And a cane? What could have happened?

Becca resisted the urge to pull Noah closer. Cling to him for all she was worth. How could she have forgotten…

This woman was Noah's grandmother.

"So, where did you put it?" the older woman asked him.

He shrugged his shoulders. "It might be in the room," he mumbled, distracted by a child sitting in a cart passing them. The little boy was licking an orange pumpkin-shaped sucker and eyeing Noah.

"The room?" Clearly puzzled, Mrs. Mitchell looked at Becca. "Where are you staying?"

"Mommy, I'm hungry," Noah whined, and Becca couldn't have been happier for the interruption.

"I know. But you need to keep your voice down, and what have I told you about interrupting grown-ups when they're talking?"

Noah muttered an apology, though he was far more interested in keeping track of the lollipop.

"I'm so sorry, Mrs. Mitchell, but it was a long drive and I really should go feed him so he can take a nap."

"Don't you worry. I understand all too well. This one here," she said, inclining her head at Ryder as he helped her straighten, "he would've eaten twenty-four seven if I'd let him. I doubt he ever went long enough between snacks to be hungry. And mind you, it lasted until he left for college."

"Oh, please don't tell me that," Becca said, laughing. "My food bill is already more than my rent."

"Come on, Mom, let's go," Ryder said. "She needs to feed the boy."

"I really do." Becca smiled. "But it was so nice seeing you, Mrs. Mitchell. And you, Ryder."

He didn't respond. She wasn't surprised. Something had triggered his apparent disdain for her. Did he think she should've dragged Amy here under protest?

"For heaven's sake, you're an adult now. Call me Gail. How long will you be here? I'd love to have you come to the ranch for a visit."

Ryder had gotten his mom moving. She'd taken a few steps but stopped, waiting for Becca's answer. Ryder's piercing stare was unreadable. Regardless, if Gail wasn't there, Becca didn't doubt that she and Ryder would be having an entirely different conversation.

"I'll call you tomorrow," Becca told her. "How's that?"

Gail's face lit up. "You still have the number?"

Becca nodded.

"Oh, and where is it that you're staying?"

"At the motel," Noah announced before Becca could stop him. "There's a elevato and I get to push the buttons."

His words tended to run together when he was excited. Becca supposed it was too much to hope that they hadn't caught the first part.

"The motel?" Gail looked to her for confirmation.

Even Ryder seemed interested.

"Gail?" The shrill voice came from somewhere behind Becca. "Yoo-hoo, over here." The woman waiting at the deli counter was waving frantically. "Don't go anywhere. I need to talk to you."

"Oh, it's Irma." Mrs. Mitchell didn't seem pleased.

"Mommy, that lady intrumted," Noah said with a mischievous grin.

"I know." Becca stifled a smile. What a little imp. "Now, say goodbye."

Gail's chuckle did nothing to erase her troubled expression. "We'll talk tomorrow," she said. "In the meantime, I'm going to throw something out that I'd like you to really think about. We've got a lot of room at the ranch and you're welcome to stay with us. In fact, I would love it. A motel is no place for an active young boy."

Ryder's jaw tightened and he pinned her with a hard stare. Clearly he didn't share his mom's enthusiasm. He'd be relieved to know Becca wouldn't accept the offer. Not in a million years.

THE NEXT MORNING, Becca and Noah went down to the lobby to check out the complimentary continental breakfast. Everything from the locally made muffins and cinnamon buns to the bowls of fresh fruit looked amazing. They even offered two varieties of dry cereal. Eating breakfast here every day would give her pocketbook a small boost.

She poured some orange juice and a glass of milk for Noah, and filled a mug of coffee for herself. Of course he had eyes only for the sweets. Becca picked out an apple and a banana and let him have half a cinnamon bun as a special treat.

Patty, the woman behind the front desk, had kindly loaned her a tray so she could carry everything back to their room. Patty had even grabbed a couple of oranges from the back and set them on the tray with a second cinnamon bun despite Becca's protest.

Ten minutes later, sitting at the small table across from Noah, Becca had finished the bun and her coffee. How could she have forgotten Marge's cinnamon rolls? Back when she and Amy were teenagers, they'd gone to Marge's Diner for the sweet gooey buns at least once a week.

The pleasant memory faded in seconds. Becca checked her phone, even knowing it was useless. Still nothing from Amy. Derek's call had chipped away some of Becca's hope, but not all of it.

Glancing up, she saw a little arm slowly reaching across the table. "Noah, stop. Finish your banana."

"No. I want *that*," he said, pointing a sticky finger at the other half of the bun, which she'd already wrapped up in a napkin.

"I said you could have half."

"No!"

"Don't yell. Drink your milk."

His cheeks growing pink, he stuck out his lower lip, and she prayed a tantrum wasn't brewing.

She'd always limited his sugar intake, for the usual health reasons, but also to temper his intermittent outbursts. Isabella had assured her that Noah was no different from any other four-year-old, but that didn't stop Becca from worrying. She wanted to believe Amy, who swore she hadn't done any drugs while she was pregnant. In fact, her addiction hadn't taken hold until after Noah was born. Still, Becca would be a fool to dismiss the possibility.

Fortunately, Noah's pout gave way to a big yawn.

Neither of them had slept well last night. Becca knew

exactly what had made her restless, but she had expected Noah to conk out.

Before she got lost in thoughts of Ryder and Gail and how she would handle the phone call that she'd promised to make, she rose and went around the table to Noah's side.

She crouched down and slipped her arms around him. "I love you, sweet boy."

"Love you, too, Mommy."

She leaned back to look at him. "What do you think about taking a nap?"

His dark blue eyes turned stormy. So much like Ryder's yesterday that her heart rate doubled. God, she wished she'd never seen the similarity.

"I'm going to lie down, too. I was hoping we could take a nap together."

Noah frowned, clearly trying to decide if he liked the idea or not.

"Then later, when we wake up, we'll go for a drive. There are all kinds of horses and cows around here."

His face brightened. "Where?"

"Not too far from town."

"Can we pet them?"

"Maybe," she said, using his napkin to wipe the corner of his mouth. "Finish your milk and banana, okay?"

"Okay," he said, drawing out the word into a sigh as he picked up his plastic cup.

Becca got to her feet and cleared the table, making sure she hid the remaining half of the cinnamon roll where he couldn't see it. Maybe they'd split it later.

"Can we ride the horses?" Noah asked, setting down his empty cup and wiping his mouth with the back of his hand.

"Horses are very big. And you don't know how to ride."

"Do you?"

Becca nodded. "It's been a long time, though."

"Will you teach me?"

"We'll see," she said, knowing that wouldn't happen. "Go wash your face and hands, please."

After putting out the Do-Not-Disturb sign, she pulled back the sheets she'd tidied earlier and fluffed Noah's pillow. He left the bathroom and headed straight for the bed, not grumbling once. But he didn't close his eyes until she joined him.

She hadn't tried to trick him. She welcomed sleep: twenty minutes, a half hour, three hours, whatever she could get. It didn't take long for the guilt and fear to sink their teeth into her. Forgetting that Noah wasn't hers by blood was much easier when she wasn't staring his grandmother and uncle in the face.

In the plus column, Becca knew returning to Blackfoot Falls had been the right thing to do. Here, she was spared the fear that Derek might suddenly show up and drag Noah away. Aside from the Mitchells, and worrying about Amy, her other problem had to do with work.

Her boss was a nice guy but his patience extended only so far. And she needed a paycheck. Soon. Just because she'd left LA didn't mean she didn't have to pay her rent. And Isabella, God bless her, had refused the money Becca had tried to give her since it wasn't her fault she wouldn't be needed for a week…or two. But Becca preferred to be optimistic.

Later, she figured she'd go take a look at her grandparents' house. See what kind of shape it was in. Thinking about the modest homestead surrounded by blue sky and open space calmed her. Her pulse had slowed and her eyelids drooped. She snuggled into the pillow and started to drift off…

A knock at the door jarred her awake. She looked over at Noah. Thankfully he hadn't moved.

She leaped out of bed and raced to the door. Forestalling a second knock, Becca skipped the peephole and pulled the door open. "Ryder?"

He took off his Stetson and ran a hand through his sandy-brown hair. "I hope this isn't too early."

"Um, no." Her heart pounded, and for a second she considered telling him it was a bad time. But not knowing what he wanted would drive her crazy. She glanced back at Noah, who still hadn't stirred. "Come in," she whispered, stepping aside to let him pass. "We'll have to keep our voices down."

As Ryder crossed the threshold, he saw Noah curled up in the middle of the bed. "I can come back later."

The faint scent of leather and saddle soap drifted in with him, bringing with it memories of long ago afternoons, her hanging out in the stables with him and his dad, asking endless questions. Until now she hadn't fully appreciated how patient they'd been with her.

"Now is better," she said. "We're going for a drive later."

"I'd hate to wake him."

"He'll be okay. We don't exactly live in the quietest neighborhood in LA." She led him to the table, suddenly conscious of her sloppy gray sweatpants and her oversize black sweatshirt sans bra. Not that he'd notice. Anyway, she was too nervous to care. He hadn't smiled once and she couldn't imagine what was so important that he'd show up unannounced like this.

She sat in the same chair she'd used earlier, and he took Noah's. The table was small but perfectly adequate…

until Ryder rested his elbows on the wood veneer surface and leaned across it. Her first impulse was to scoot her chair back. Then she realized he'd leaned close so as not to disturb Noah.

A flicker of amusement relaxed his features. "I woke you. Sorry."

"No," she said, her hand going to her messy hair. "I was just trying to get Noah to—" Becca sighed. She had a pretty good idea what she looked like. "I might've drifted off."

"This won't take long," he murmured in a pitch so low she had to lean forward to hear him. "Have you thought about my mom's offer?"

Becca should've known why he'd come. "Yes, I have. And the answer is no, we won't be staying at your ranch. So you don't have to worry about it."

A wry half grin rested on his well-shaped mouth. "I want you to take her up on it."

"Why?"

"Come on, Becca, are we really going to do this?"

"Do what?"

He stared silently back at her, though not as if he were considering the question. Ryder looked as he had yesterday. Just plain disgusted.

Pretending to check on Noah, she turned her head. Between Amy's lies and Becca's guilt over believing the worst about him, and of course, the biggie—the secret she was keeping from the Mitchells—it was difficult for her to keep all the confusing emotions in check. No telling what her face was giving away.

Something else occurred to her. If Amy had lied to her, she'd probably lied to her family. About what, though?

Chapter Five

Ryder watched a flush creep across Becca's cheeks as she briefly met his eyes. Guilt, no doubt. Which was fitting. If she hadn't manipulated Amy into running off with her, his sister would have probably married Billy, whose folks owned the Circle K. She would've settled down right there in Blackfoot Falls and given their mom a couple of grandbabies by now.

Something Ryder had failed to do.

Damn, he couldn't let that line of thinking sabotage him. He'd already wasted too much time steeped in regret, wondering how everything in his marriage had gone so wrong.

Becca hadn't said a word. And now that she'd turned back to look at her son, Ryder couldn't read her.

He'd never had a problem doing that when she was a kid. Back then, when she'd followed him around with big puppy dog eyes, her expression could tell a whole story. His mom had threatened to ground him for a year if he said one word to embarrass her.

At the time he'd been twenty-one, too old to be grounded, but he hadn't done anything to make her feel awkward. He'd liked Becca. She'd had a healthy respect for horses and ranching in general. Except for that year after her mom had moved to Alaska with her new husband. Becca had practically transformed overnight.

When she stubbornly refused to look at him again, he asked, "Does the kid have a father?"

"He has a name. It's Noah," she said, turning back to Ryder with a fire in her eyes he hadn't seen before. "I didn't use a sperm donor, if that's what you're asking."

He almost smiled. "Are you married?"

At first, she just stared at him. "How is that your business?"

"It's not."

She blinked. "How about you and Leanne? You must have kids by now."

Ryder winced a little. "We're divorced."

"Oh. I'm sorry."

"It happens."

"Any kids?"

He shook his head.

Becca sighed. "I'm not married. Never have been. It's just Noah and me."

Ryder turned to look at the boy snuggled under the covers. "He's a cute kid."

"He is." Her lips lifted in a gentle smile, then all of a sudden her guard went up.

Ryder hadn't said or done anything to provoke it. Yet the barrier between them was so obvious it was almost tangible.

"Frankly, I don't understand why you'd want us around," she said. "You certainly didn't hide your feelings yesterday."

"All right. While we're being *frank*," he said, and she blinked at his mocking tone, "I think you know something about Amy you aren't telling us."

"I don't even know where she is. And that's the truth."

"What do you mean?"

Becca sighed. "I don't know how to say it any plainer than that."

"Noah said she gave him a toy."

"Yes. When she came by my place last week, but I haven't seen her since. I've tried calling her cell but she hasn't answered."

"You guys don't share a place?"

"Not for a few years. She lives with her boyfriend."

Ryder heard a trace of scorn in her voice, saw her tense. Clearly she didn't like the guy, he thought, then noticed the tiny quiver at the corner of her mouth. No, it was more than dislike. She was afraid. "Tell me about this boyfriend of hers."

Crossing her arms over her chest, she hunched her shoulders. "I don't know him, not really. I'm not a fan so Amy doesn't bring him around."

"You know enough to dislike him. What is it about him that you—?"

"Look, ask Amy, okay? It's her business. I won't discuss it with you."

"I'd be more than happy to ask her if she'd ever bother calling. Or if she would give us her damn number. Did you know we haven't heard from her in a year? And that she blocked her number?"

"Keep it down. You're going to wake Noah."

"Come on, Becca. Work with me here. You look worried, so naturally now I'm concerned."

She briefly closed her eyes. "I'm sorry," she said, rubbing her right temple.

He waited for her to continue. And got nothing. "Guess I should've listened to my gut. Hell, I can still drive down there. How many hours did it take you?"

"No." Eyes wide, she stared at him. "Don't. Please."

Ryder felt a sinking sensation in the pit of his stomach. "You want to tell me why I shouldn't?" he said. "Because I gotta say, by the look on your face, I'm thinking I should've left a week ago."

"Please, Ryder." She reached across the table and clutched his hand. "Amy's leaving him. She might've done it already."

"The boyfriend?"

She nodded. "If you show up, it'll make things worse."

That made no sense at all. Something sure had rattled her. She hadn't let go of his hand. In fact, she was squeezing tighter, though he doubted she was aware of it.

"Look, if you'd just tell me the truth," he said, "maybe I can help."

Becca blinked, then looked at her fingers curling over his hand, her fingernails digging into his palm. Her eyes widened a fraction. Oh, yeah, she was rattled. She hadn't even figured out he'd been bluffing. How could he *show up* when he didn't even know where Amy lived?

Straightening her spine, Becca slowly withdrew her hand. She clasped it with her other one. "I've told you the truth. I can't help it if you choose not to believe me."

"Fair enough. But now I've got another problem. Going by what you just told me, I have to believe you know exactly where Amy is, you know what kind of trouble she's in, and yet you left her behind to fend for herself."

Becca's faint smile was tinged with bitterness. "You obviously don't know your sister very well."

"How could I? She was still a kid when you dragged her to LA."

The smile vanished. Her eyes filled with disbelief as her lips parted. He could see her mind working. She'd probably tell him to go to hell, which wouldn't be entirely undeserved—Amy had always been headstrong. But he knew Amy hadn't been keen on going to LA because she'd told him so. She'd gone for Becca's sake.

After several moments of charged silence, Becca pushed back in her chair and stood. "Well, I believe we've said all there is to say, so if you'll excuse me…we have a full day planned."

"You haven't answered me."

"Oh, was there a question in there?" She hadn't bothered to keep her voice down. Apparently she'd rather wake her son than have to finish their conversation. "It sounded more like an accusation."

Her expression startled him.

She wasn't just angry. Becca looked hurt. Hell, what did she expect? She had a lot of nerve to show up and pretend she didn't have news of Amy. Then to admit she'd deserted his sister. He saw her hand tremble slightly. No. No way. He wouldn't feel sorry for her.

He thought back to yesterday at the Food Mart. The way his mom had fawned over her had pissed him off. The memory put him to rights. If Becca was upset, it was her own doing.

"Look," he said, "how about we call a truce?"

"I have no quarrel with you. Anyway, I doubt we'll run into each other again."

He bit back a curse. "You promised to call my mom."

"And I will." She walked past him, waving a hand as if she were dismissing him.

Ryder caught her wrist. "Don't wake the boy yet. We need to settle this first." He moved his thumb against her inner wrist. So soft.

She glared at him. "Let me go."

He released her and cleared his throat. "Look, I'm asking you on behalf of my mother."

"Did she send you?"

"She doesn't know I'm here, and I'd prefer to keep it that way."

"I won't say anything." Becca absently rubbed her wrist.

His grip hadn't been tight enough to hurt her. Was she trying to play him? Good luck. He'd run low on sympathy long before today. Unfortunately, he could tell she wasn't going to accept his mom's invitation.

"Come on, be smart. Staying at the Sundowner means you'd save some money." Unlike Becca, he continued to keep his voice low. "And Noah would have lots of space and plenty to occupy him. Don't let how we feel about each other influence your decision. You'd hardly see me."

Her brows rose. "How we feel about each other? I hadn't given you a single thought before yesterday."

"If I recall, neither of us were exactly overjoyed."

"Oh." She blushed and looked away. "Right. Anyway, moot point."

Ryder wondered about the sudden awkwardness, then remembered Amy teasing him about Becca having a crush on him. But that had been kid stuff, at least ten years ago. Something else was bothering her.

She stood beside the bed where Noah was curled up, gazing down at her son with so much heart it stopped him in his tracks. Whatever her faults, she certainly loved that child. With no husband in the picture and living in an expensive city like LA? Maybe the kid's father helped out some, but Ryder had the feeling that wasn't the case. Either way, he gave her credit.

"Wait," he said when she was about to wake the boy. She was a mother. He knew how to appeal to her. "I doubt Amy told you. She might not even know since her calls had dropped off, but my mom had a stroke."

"Oh, no. When?"

"A couple years ago."

"I wondered about the cane. I'm really sorry. Despite…everything, I've always liked your mom. A lot. Your father, too. They were both nice to me." She winced. "Even after my mom left and I wasn't at my best."

Ryder laughed. "That's one way of putting it."

"Hey, I could've been worse."

Noah stirred.

Ryder hurried on. "After seeing you and Noah yesterday, she was the happiest I've seen her in years. As soon as we got home, she started freshening up the guest rooms and writing out meal plans…"

Becca briefly nibbled at her lower lip, eyeing him suspiciously. "Playing dirty, are we?"

"Just telling it like it is."

She hesitated, then turned back to her son. "Noah? Time to wake up, sleepyhead."

Ryder sighed. So she was willing to use the kid to avoid answering? Fine.

Noah jerked his head up with a start. He blinked, looked around, but didn't see Becca behind him. He rubbed both eyes with small fists and immediately started to cry.

"Hey, Mr. Cranky Pants…" Placing a hand on his shoulder, she sat on the edge of the bed. "I'm right here."

Those weren't crocodile tears. He looked genuinely afraid until he turned and buried his face against his mom's chest. She held him close and stroked his back. "It's okay, sweetie. We're in the motel with the elevator you like to ride, remember?"

Her voice was soft and soothing as she rocked the boy back and forth. Watching and listening to her, even Ryder felt as if he was being drawn into her spell. Her brown hair fell in waves just past her shoulders, the sunlight coming through the window picking up the coppery highlights she'd hated as a kid. Easy to forget the gawky teenager he'd known had become this very attractive woman.

The boy's sobs slowly turned to hiccups. Then a few sniffles as Becca dried his cheeks with her thumb and the sleeve of her sweatshirt. She gave him a tender smile. "Everything okay?"

Her son nodded.

"Hey, Noah," Ryder said quietly. "Remember me?"

The boy looked at him and nodded again.

Becca's fierce frown might've made a lesser man back off.

Ryder briefly met her gaze, then asked Noah, "Did your mom tell you about all the horses we have at our ranch?"

The boy's eyes rounded. "Real ones?"

"You bet."

"Do you have white horses?"

"Yep. My favorite is Jethro. He has a big bushy mane and tail."

Noah wrinkled his nose. "What's a mane?"

Ryder turned all the way around in his chair. He didn't have to look at Becca to know she was shooting daggers. "You know all that stuff on their neck and back that kind of looks like hair?" he asked, and Noah nodded vigorously. "That's called a mane."

"Do you have other color horses?"

"We do. Brown, black, spotted. Big horses, small ones. And you know what?"

The boy's eyes glowed with excitement. "What?"

"You and your mom might be staying with us at the ranch, so you'll get to see all the horses you want."

"Mommy?" He turned to Becca. She quickly produced a smile. "Can we, Mommy?"

Watching as she swept Noah's hair away from his eyes, Ryder studied her. He'd figured she'd be pissed at him, not that he would blame her. Using the kid was a sneaky way to hedge his bet. But for a minute, she'd looked upset. More like panicked. What the hell was that about?

"I think we can work in a short visit later," she said finally.

"But Ryder said we can stay there."

"You know what, sweetie? I want you to call him Mr. Mitchell, okay? He's a grown-up." She sent him a quick glare and muttered, "Even when he doesn't act like one."

Noah frowned. "Can I call him Uncle Ryder? Like how I call Aunt Amy?"

The color seemed to drain from Becca's face. Her lips parted, but nothing came out.

"I like the sound of that," Ryder said. "Call me Uncle Ryder."

Noah grinned. "I want to see *all* the horses," he said and jumped off the bed.

Becca caught the back of his shirt. "Wait a minute. Go brush your teeth."

"I did already."

"Not after you ate breakfast."

"Okay," Noah drawled and plodded toward the bathroom. A few seconds later, Ryder heard the water running.

His gaze stayed on Becca, who hadn't quite recovered since her son had mentioned Amy. Distrust rose inside of him until he could almost taste it.

"Is there something you want to tell me?" he asked, keeping his voice low and even.

She glanced toward the open bathroom door. The

water from the sink was running while Noah hummed. "You're a bastard."

Ryder just smiled—despite the fact he was still bothered by her earlier reaction. And something else that troubled him… He'd noticed she wasn't wearing a bra.

Chapter Six

The gravel road that led to the Sundowner Ranch loomed ten yards ahead. Becca could have found it in her sleep. Gripping the steering wheel with one hand, she dragged the other clammy palm down her jeans.

It didn't matter how many times she'd told herself this was the perfect opportunity to see the Mitchells with fresh eyes. If it wasn't for Noah, buckled up in his car seat in the back of her old compact, she would've given in to the urge to keep on driving instead of making the turn.

"Real horses, Mommy. Do you think they have a pony like at the park? You said I could ride one when I was bigger, and I'm a lot bigger than when I was three."

"I don't know about ponies, Noah, but you can ask Mr. Mitchell if they have any foals."

"You mean Uncle Ryder?"

Grimacing, Becca bit down hard and caught the edge of her lip. "Yes," she said, telling herself it was fine. Calling him *Uncle* meant nothing. Just as long as she didn't make a big deal out of it.

"What's a foal?"

"A baby horse." When the tires hit gravel, her foot eased off the pedal as her heart rate jumped. She knew this road far too well. She'd walked from her grandparents' house many times when she was a kid, whatever the weather. Well, not when it stormed, but she'd had a great big red bubble coat that Grandpa had said made her look like the Marshmallow Man with a sunburn.

And when it was autumn, like now, she and Amy would go off the road and shuffle through the colored leaves, kicking and talking and making plans for when they were older.

None of those plans had come true.

Then when she was twelve, Ryder had taught her to ride, and like a big dope, she'd developed a crush on him. She'd spent hours fantasizing about how he'd be a good husband and daddy, unlike her own father, who'd always put his army career first. She and Ryder would live in a house right between her grandparents and the Mitchells, ranching and riding horses all day long. He'd been nineteen at the time. She wondered if he'd known about her crush and had laughed at her behind her back.

"Mommy?"

"Yes, sweetie?"

"Did the car break?"

She'd stopped, her thoughts stalled on a life she'd never have. And heaven knew, she'd never once imagined Ryder hating her. Even though she'd hated him for so many years.

Even now, knowing that Amy had lied, Becca still struggled to remember he wasn't the man Amy had painted so vividly. Hard to believe Amy had never gotten any work as an actress. She sure had been convincing.

Oh, Amy.

Despite everything, Becca could barely think about her without feeling a little sick. Amy still hadn't called, and the not-knowing was eating at Becca. Maybe she was okay, just not ready to face the music now that she knew Becca knew the truth.

"The car is fine, Noah. I was just being careful not to hit anything."

"Like horses?"

"Yeah. We'll be there soon."

"Good. I need to pee."

She sighed. "Can you hold it for a few more minutes?"

"I think so."

That, if nothing else, got her to move them along regardless of her trepidation. She'd spoken to Mrs. Mitchell—calling her Gail was going to be hard—after Ryder had left. Well, not right away. He'd pissed her off royally by using Noah and making her the bad guy if she said no.

But since this visit was for his mom, Becca had decided she wouldn't let Ryder's sneaky tactics influence her. At least she'd had the fortitude to tell Gail straight off that they would only be staying one night. But then she'd remembered the stroke, and how Gail had responded to Noah, and Becca had hinted at a second night. And that's where she'd put her foot down.

Two nights, max, then back to the motel where she could keep a clear head. Not that it would be easy to leave once Noah got a load of all the horses.

"Is it a few minutes yet?"

"Not quite. If you look straight ahead, you'll see the big sign that tells us we're entering the Sundowner."

"What's that?"

"The name of the Mitchells' ranch."

"Whoa…that sign is really high up," Noah said as they got closer. "Do you think they had to stand on a horse to put it up there?"

"I don't know. That's something else you can ask—your uncle."

She wanted to take back the flip suggestion. The more

time Noah spent with Ryder, the more likely it was Noah would say something that would make things even more awkward. Or she would.

Becca got her first glimpse of the two-story house on the hill, the one that looked out over the property. It seemed larger than what she remembered and must have had a new coat of paint since she'd seen it last. In fact, there was a second barn now, and several newer outbuildings had replaced the older ones where she and Amy had hung out. She wasn't even sure what they all were, except for the big white bunkhouse, which still looked like something out of a Western movie.

By the time they got up to the first corral, Noah was pretty much hyperventilating. It was clear this was no petting zoo. Men were on horses, the cattle were lowing like a full orchestra, and, oh, man, that was Wiley. As lean as always and still walked like he was gonna be late.

She wondered if Otis was around and running the bunkhouse. He used to let them churn the big old-fashioned ice cream bucket during the summer months. Gail would bring in fresh peaches or strawberries, and they'd crank that sucker until it felt as if their arms would fall off. But they got the first two servings for their labor.

"Do they have baby goats, you think? Mommy? Like we saw? And baby ducks?"

"I think they mostly have cows and horses, Noah."

"Is that the house where we'll sleep tonight?"

"It is." She pulled up next to an older truck that was parked near the path to the house. The front garden was almost all dormant, even though the weather had been mild compared to past Novembers. But the trees that bracketed the stone walkway were gorgeous, the ground beneath them covered in red and gold leaves.

Becca's stomach clenched as she shut off the engine,

wondering if she shouldn't just flat out confess to every last thing that had happened since she and Amy had left. But losing Noah? It would be like tearing her heart from her chest. Not to mention what it would do to him.

He was only four, and he'd only known one mommy. She couldn't just walk away from him, not when she knew all too well what it felt like to watch her own mother walk away.

Hell, her mom didn't even know about Noah. It wasn't that they never talked, but it seemed Katie had a knack for calling when Becca was at work and couldn't talk long. A good thing, actually, since Becca hadn't known what to tell her about Noah, not while everything had been up in the air with Amy.

Anyway, Katie hadn't been all that interested in news from LA. Not when she had so many tales of her own, such as watching the glaciers slowly disappearing and the wildlife threatened. These days, Katie was all about protecting the land and the wild things…not her only daughter.

Becca had to hurry and get out to unbuckle Noah before he had a fit. It was no surprise that he was over-excited. This was a big deal to him.

"Can we go see the horses? Can we?"

"I thought you had to use the bathroom."

"But I can do that super fast. Then can we go see them?"

"Stop squirming so I can get you out of this seat." It took him a few seconds to settle. "Okay," she said as she continued to unbuckle him. "First, we're going to be good guests. Remember how we talked about that?"

"Say please and thank you," he said, drawing the words out to a sigh. "Ask nicely and don't grab."

"That's right. And what are you going to say to Mrs. Mitchell when we go inside?"

"Thank you for inviting us, Mrs. Mitchell."

"Good boy. All right, we'll deal with our bags later. Let's make sure we don't have any accidents first."

Once he was free, he wasn't sure which way to go, so he jumped up and down, so anxious he could barely contain himself.

She took hold of his hand, and he hopped all the way up the long stone pathway, up to the big old porch that still had the double swing on the right and the pair of rockers on the left. But there were two new benches, and the formerly brown shutters were now a rich green.

Before Becca could knock on the door, it swung open, and there was Gail, leaning on her cane. Her face lit up as if it were her birthday and she'd just gotten the gift of her dreams.

Becca pulled a smile from somewhere and could only hope the overwhelming sadness of what she knew and couldn't say didn't show in her eyes.

"Welcome back, sweetheart," Gail said, pulling her into another hug. "I've missed you so."

"Me, too," Becca said, an inconvenient lump making her voice thick while she struggled to swallow.

The moment Gail turned her attention to Noah, her blue eyes sparkled. "And how are you, Noah?"

"Thanks for inviting us, Mrs. Mitchell," he said, racing to get it all out. *Mitchell* ended up more of a mumble than a word right before he blurted out, "I have to pee."

Gail laughed. Hard. And that's when Becca saw Ryder. He wasn't looking at her. Couldn't be. Not with that kind of a smile.

Putting a hand on his mother's shoulder, he gave it a

gentle squeeze. "It's been too long since I've heard that sound."

Gail patted his hand. "Why don't you show our young guest here to the bathroom while Becca and I go see about lunch."

Ryder finally leveled his gaze at Becca, dropping his smile in favor of a look that said it all: *I don't like you. I don't trust you. I don't want you here. But I'll tolerate you for my mother's sake.*

It only lasted for a few seconds, but it felt as if she'd been scalded.

"Come on, Noah." Ryder held out his hand. "Let's get you taken care of so we can go out to the stable."

Noah hopped up and down, his eyes wild with excitement. "Horses, horses, horses. Now!"

"Oh, please don't do that," Becca said, horrified that he'd have an accident right there on the porch. She caught hold of his arm. "Thanks for the offer," she said, glancing at Ryder, "but I think for the first time in a strange house, I should take him."

"Oh, goodness, of course you should," Gail said, stepping back to give them room. "It's been some time since I've had little ones around."

Noah shook away her hand. "No."

"Noah? What did we talk about?" Becca narrowed her eyes in warning. "You and I will go together so I can help you," she said and when he stuck out his lower lip, she crouched beside him. "This bathroom might not look like the one at home. Remember how we stopped at the gas station and it was a little scary?"

Noah's frown hadn't eased.

"I'm sorry," Becca said, feeling self-conscious and glancing up. It struck her then that Noah, with his small arms folded, was mimicking Ryder.

"Look," Ryder said, "I'm sure I can manage to help him out if need be."

"Okay." Becca shrugged and stood up. "If you don't mind a blow-by-blow account of what's happening while he sits on the john."

The crease between Ryder's brows deepened as he thought about it. Now, his frown matched Noah's.

Gail let out a laugh. "I forgot about those days. Ryder was so funny. He used to—"

"All right. That's enough." Ryder rubbed his jaw. Underneath his tanned skin, Becca thought he'd flushed a bit. "Come on, buddy. Go with your mom, then after, we can go see the horses."

"Yay! Horses!" Noah was all smiles again.

Becca tried not to resent how easily *Uncle Ryder* had turned Noah's mood around.

Having her hand tugged reminded Becca that she'd better hurry. "Down the hallway, first door on the right?"

Gail nodded, looking pleased. "You remember."

"Well, I was here practically every day."

"Mommy. Come on." Noah tugged harder and she almost bumped into Ryder.

He didn't move, just stood there, tall and broad in a snug T-shirt, muscled arms crossed over his chest.

Ignoring him, she let Noah pull her along, hoping he didn't have an accident on the way. He didn't very often, but when he was this excited, he sometimes waited too long.

Even in their rush, Becca couldn't help but notice the house had changed. The furnishings were more streamlined, definitely lighter. Gail had always admired the Shaker approach, and it showed in the simple but perfect antiques that were artfully placed in the large living room. The hallway, what little she could see before they reached the bathroom, had been made into a picture wall.

"Mommy?" Noah looked up at her, his hand on the doorknob. "I can go by myself, but stay right here if I call you."

"You sure?"

He nodded.

"Don't close the door all the way."

"Okay."

Becca's gaze drifted back to the wall. The photo closest to her was of Amy at about thirteen, striking a pose. She'd always played to the camera. Such a ham. Next to that one was a picture of Mr. Mitchell sitting atop Tonto, a roan gelding that had been a favorite of his. Odd that Becca had remembered the horse's name.

Or maybe not. She really had spent half her childhood at the Sundowner, listening to music with Amy in her room or eating dinner with the family or pestering whoever had been in the stable at the time.

Peering closer at Mr. Mitchell, she wondered when the photo had been taken. With his endless patience, he'd taught her more about horses than anyone else, except for Ryder.

Yet she hadn't come back for his funeral. She hadn't said goodbye. Instead, she'd let herself believe everything Amy had told her. If the lies were the reason Amy hadn't called her yet, that would hurt just as much. Didn't Amy realize Becca would end up forgiving her in time?

Becca felt the sting of tears and breathed in deeply. Not now.

God, please, not now.

She exhaled slowly. Blinked away an errant tear. Dabbed at her cheek just in case.

Moving closer to the bathroom door, she listened for a moment. “Noah? You okay?”

“Yes, Mommy.”

When she turned back to the photos, she saw Ryder standing at the end of the hall, watching her.

Chapter Seven

Just as Ryder walked out of the house, he realized he should've grabbed a jacket. He'd known the air was chilly but he'd been too distracted.

Logic told him that hanging on to his bitterness toward Becca didn't serve his purpose. So far, that hadn't stopped him from resenting the hell out of her. And she could get choked up looking at photos all she wanted; it didn't mean he'd feel any sympathy for her.

The bottom line, though, was that he'd asked her to come to the Sundowner for the sake of his mom, and that was what he needed to remember. He just wished she'd stayed in the kitchen instead of following him and Noah to the stable as if she was afraid to have the kid out of her sight for one lousy second. What did she think he was going to do to the boy?

"Noah, wait for us before you go inside that stable." She walked just ahead of Ryder, while Noah ran as fast as his little legs could carry him.

Becca hurried to reach him, her hips swaying subtly in those tight worn jeans. She sure had come a long way from being that thin, awkward teenager who'd followed him around, hoping he'd let her go for a horseback ride.

"The stable's different," she said, turning to face

Ryder. When she realized he'd been trailing her by only a couple feet, she stepped back.

"We had some problems with the roof on the old stable, and it was too small. So we built this one."

"I noticed the changes in the house as well. I can see that it's easier for your mom to maneuver with the walker."

"Yeah. She uses the cane most of the time. But some days are worse than others."

"I still can't believe she had a stroke. She's too young. It must have been devastating."

Ryder slowed. "It would have been better if her daughter had been here." He waited, not sure what he was hoping for.

"Uncle Ryder, hurry!"

"Hold your horses," he said, as he picked up the pace.

"Hold a horse?" The boy was jumping again. Was it a Noah thing, or just a four-year-old thing? He'd been around kids, but not a lot of them and not for long stretches. For his mom's sake, he planned on seeing that this one stayed around as long as possible.

He just wished Noah didn't come with all that baggage. But remembering how his mom's face had brightened at the sight of the boy, Ryder was willing to forget a lot.

Noah stopped at the entrance to the stable. Ryder had figured the lure of what was inside would tempt the boy to disobey, but Noah had stuck to the rules.

"Now," Ryder said, crouching down beside Noah. The rich smell of fresh hay mingled with the less fragrant scents of the animals behind him. "Horses are pretty big, but they're real friendly, as long as there's not a lot of jumping and loud noise. That can make a horse nervous. You think you can remember that while we go meet them?"

Noah aborted his next jump halfway through and curled his hands into fists as he stood perfectly still. "Yes."

"Good. I'll let you know when you can pet them, okay?"

The boy nodded and stayed calm until they were in the stable proper where he got a load of all the stalls. From there, he could see just how big the horses were. Being four, that had to be intimidating. Noah started to twitch.

Becca slid into position beside her son. She ran her fingers up into his straight brown hair, scratching lightly with her neat beige nails. Noah relaxed inch by inch. His shoulders first, fists last.

It made the hair on the back of Ryder's neck stand up. For a second, it had felt as if she was doing that to him, running those fingers from his nape to his crown. Which was crazy. He'd had women's fingers in his hair before. From casual dates to his ex-wife. None of them had made him— "So, you ready to go meet the horses?"

Noah's "Yes!" was louder than Ryder had expected. He was sure none of the horses were spooked, but he'd jerked a bit.

"Inside voice, Noah." Becca stepped back, letting Ryder take the lead.

They walked over to the first stall. "This big guy is named Maverick. He's twelve years old and he really likes carrots."

Noah's mouth was open and his eyes went wide. "He's way big."

"Yep." Ryder ran his hand down Maverick's neck. "He's gentle as can be, and if you want, you can pet him."

Noah stepped closer to his mom. "I can't reach."

"We can fix that." Ryder scooped him up, his knuckles accidentally brushing Becca's hip.

She barely reacted, just stepped to the side as he held Noah up high enough to touch Maverick's neck. "Here," she said, moving closer now. "Stroke gently like this."

Ryder fixed his gaze on her small, slim hand as she ran it down the side of the horse's neck. Noah's tiny fingers followed his mom's lead. Maverick was one happy camper.

Ryder, on the other hand…

"Okay," he said, setting Noah down. "Why don't we go meet your mother's favorite horse?"

At his abruptness, Becca frowned.

Noah blinked, then stared at his mother as if she'd been hiding a treasure. "You got a horse?"

BECCA'S GAZE WENT from Noah to Ryder and back again. "Not exactly," she said, stunned that Ryder had remembered her infatuation with Miss Kitty, the only palomino on the ranch back then. "I used to come here a lot when Aunt Amy and I were kids, and Miss Kitty and I became friends, too."

"Did you hold him?"

"Miss Kitty's a girl horse. I got to ride her sometimes and I used to feed her apples."

"No carrots?"

"Those, too." Warmed by the pleasant memories, Becca walked over to the fourth stall where Miss Kitty whinnied, the same way she always had when Becca used to come by.

"Your mom also learned how to take care of Miss Kitty," Ryder said. "She brushed her and gave her baths."

Noah stared at Becca in awe. "Can we give her a bath?"

"She looks pretty clean to me," Becca said.

Noah's nose scrunched. "Can I see the bathtub?"

Ryder laughed, and the sound of it was enough to send her back in time. When she'd been a tween and a teenager, Ryder had laughed a lot—a low deep chuckle that had made her silly heart flutter. And then he'd smile. Like right now. As much as he despised her, he'd gone out of his way to make Noah feel welcome.

The tense feeling in her chest wasn't new. Ever since she and Amy had left Blackfoot Falls, she'd felt that squeeze to her soul. Which was one of the reasons why coming here today had been such a bad decision. Not just because of the whole mess with Amy and Noah, but because this attitude from Ryder was like being body slammed over and over again. They'd always gotten along. He'd never made fun of her, never treated her like an idiot, even when she'd done idiotic things.

Ryder leaned toward Noah, then stage-whispered, "She used to paint Miss Kitty's hooves with nail polish."

"What color?" Noah asked, turning to face Becca.

"I can't believe you remember that," she said, shaking her head at Ryder before addressing Noah. "Pink, usually. And different colors for the holidays."

"Can we do that?"

"I'm afraid not," she said, the same second Ryder said, "Sure."

Noah looked delighted. He loved pulling fast ones on Isabella, usually about cookies. Becca supposed she should be happy he hadn't yet learned to be cynical.

But she was still stuck on the fact that Ryder had remembered Miss Kitty was her favorite. And told her son.

Her son. Her heart.

His nephew.

AT A QUARTER to five, Becca was dicing the last potato near the kitchen sink while Gail browned the ground beef for the shepherd's pie. It was one of Becca's favorite meals, and Gail making it was no accident. Tonight's menu was Gail's way of asking Becca and Noah to stay longer. Somehow Amy's mother had discovered that chocolate cake was Noah's *most favorite*, aside from cookies, and two round cake pans were now cooling on the countertop.

"I wish I could understand why she stopped calling." Gail's voice cracked on the last word. "Amy and I mostly got along. Same with her dad and Ryder. She wasn't like some of the girls at that high school. You know the ones I mean."

Becca nodded as her thoughts swung back to the past. As was probably the case at most schools, there were the rebels, the outcasts and the troublemakers, along with the jocks and the prom queens. Not that Becca would ever admit it, but Amy was more of a troublemaker than Gail had known. Amy's gift was her knack for never getting caught.

Becca's hands stilled. She hoped that was still true. That Amy was somewhere in hiding, not daring to phone until the coast was completely clear. Although the odds of that were diminishing by the day.

"She never complained about home," Becca said, and that had been true, until she'd "poured her heart out" to her best friend and lied through her teeth.

"I know she hated living out here in the boonies," Gail said. "I'm not shocked that she wanted to go to Los Angeles, but she promised to keep in touch. To come back for holidays and special occasions."

Becca knew she should say something, she just didn't know what. "She misses you. We talk about you a lot," she said finally, only to realize a split second later that she'd just opened a can of worms. So she rushed on, "But living in a big city kind of caught us both off guard. It was so expensive. At least she's done well bartending. It sure pays more than I made as a waitress."

"I worry, though. As far as I know, she never used to drink and now..." Gail sighed. "Please, forgive me. I promised myself I wouldn't put you in a difficult situation. Let's change the subject."

Becca didn't argue. She'd expected to be asked tricky questions, and she'd dreaded them more than anything. Even worse, they made her think about Amy and what Derek might've done—

Her throat threatened to close up on her, which couldn't happen. Quickly, she dumped the potatoes in a pot of water and put them on to boil. "Mrs. M—Gail, if you don't mind, I'd like to go check on Noah."

"Yes, of course, I'd hate for him to wake up in a strange bedroom alone. Go. I can finish up." Gail got busy with seasonings, and Becca stopped to take the peas and carrots out of the freezer, grateful she had an excuse to go and pull herself together.

"I'll be right back," she said, touching Gail's arm as she left the big, airy kitchen. With the exception of the new stainless steel appliances, it hadn't changed much. Still yellow and white, the pantry and the fridge always full and open to whatever experiments two young girls could make a mess of.

The large garden window over the sink was, as always, covered with little pots of herbs Gail managed to keep going all year long. Becca remembered how Grams had tried to pry Gail's secret out of her, but all she'd say was that it took a little water and lots of love.

Grams's response had been, "Like hell." Becca

grinned at the memory. It was the first and only time she'd heard Grams cuss.

Huh.

She slowed her step.

It was nice, thinking about Grams without feeling depressingly sad. Becca had thought staying at the Sundowner would have the opposite effect. But mostly, this house held a lot of happy memories…before they all had come crashing down under the weight of Amy's lies.

After the shock of her written confession had worn off, the fond memories had started trickling in again. A good deal of them had come during the long drive to Montana.

One in particular had stuck out. Ryder had loved his country music back when he was a teenager, and the memory of him teaching her how to line dance was something she'd thought of several times over the years. He'd taught Amy, too, and they'd laughed themselves silly.

Nice that she could now remember those snippets of her past without feeling guilty. Without having to quash them because of the violence she'd believed he'd done to Amy. Becca used to hang out here all the time…she knew the whole family. How could she have fallen for Amy's lies? That mystery was going to haunt her for a while.

On the second floor, Becca stepped lightly as she got closer to the slightly ajar door, hoping Noah was still down for the count. He didn't nap all that often anymore, but the excitement had worn him out. Gail, knowing Becca wanted to share a room with Noah, had set them up in the larger guest room, which just so happened to be right next to Ryder's bedroom.

She'd gotten a peek of it when they'd put their bags away, and it looked so empty that it got her wondering if and when he'd moved back in. He would've been divorced by the time his dad had died. Made sense that he'd stay here so Gail wouldn't be alone.

Noah was still asleep in the queen bed. He'd cried that he wasn't tired when she tucked him in and she'd promised they could paint the horse's toes. She was almost tempted to wake him now so he'd be sure to sleep tonight, but she'd give him until the shepherd's pie was in the oven and the cake was iced.

An hour later, they were all at the table, and Ryder was pouring iced tea for his mother, while Becca tucked a napkin under Noah's chin. Everything smelled delicious. Noah still looked a little sleepy, but his appetite was raring to go.

After serving him, she took a pretty big scoop of the shepherd's pie herself, then passed the dish to Ryder. He took it without looking at her, which wasn't a surprise, just disappointing. She decided to concentrate on the moment, on Gail, and the bounty in front of her. "I can't believe how wonderful this all looks."

"You made half of it," Gail said, laughing. "I should be ashamed of myself for putting you to work. Especially with you being on your feet every day. And in a restaurant to boot."

"Actually, I work in an office now."

Gail raised her eyebrows. "You do?"

Becca chewed quickly and swallowed. "I'm still with the same steakhouse chain, but I was promoted recently."

"Now, is this the chain you worked for when you first arrived in LA?" Gail asked. "I've forgotten the name."

"Same one. I waited tables for four years, then the owner opened a new restaurant closer to my house and offered me the assistant manager position." She could feel Ryder's gaze boring into her, but he hadn't said a word.

"Then a month ago, Warren promoted me to Research and Development."

"I don't know what that means," Gail said. "But it sounds impressive."

"That's okay, I'm not sure what it means either." Becca laughed, so did Gail. Noah, who'd been eating steadily and paying them no attention, laughed along with them.

Ryder didn't even blink; he might as well have been carved from stone.

Becca wiped the corner of Noah's mouth before she continued, "Warren had three restaurants when I first started, and now he owns seven. He's looking to expand further and my job is to help determine which areas have a need for a moderately priced steakhouse and whether it would be feasible to meet the demand."

"Well, good for you." Gail's smile was full of pride.

"Frankly, I'm a little nervous since I've never done this type of work before, and I still have a lot to learn, but Warren is a smart guy. He wouldn't have promoted me if he didn't think I was up to the task."

Becca noticed Ryder's patronizing little smile but she doubted Gail had. Boy, was he lucky his mom and Noah were there, or she would've called him out.

"I know you'd planned on going to community college after high school. I imagine that helped you work your way up the ladder," Gail commented.

"Honestly, between work and Noah I haven't managed to find the time, but thanks to my new schedule, I'm really hoping to take night courses next semester. I already have my eye on two of them." She hated that Ryder's reaction still bothered her. Did he think she was being naive? Or that she was sleeping with her boss?

"I hope you follow through with that, I really do. It's hard enough being a single mom let alone holding down a job, too. You need to do something special for yourself," Gail said, tucking into her dinner for the first time since they'd sat down. "I have every faith you'll do great."

"Thank you, Gail. That means a lot." Becca wiped some gravy off Noah's chin, and then she glanced at Ryder again. His eyes had narrowed and he looked as if he didn't believe a word she'd said.

HE WASN'T BUYING IT.

After taking a sip of water, Ryder looked back at Becca, but she was talking to his mother about old friends and neighbors. Noah was gobbling his dinner with gusto, not even a little interested in the conversation.

What Ryder wanted to know was why Becca hadn't bothered to name the steakhouse chain she was so thrilled about. Or why she'd lied about Amy working at the bar. He'd overheard a little of the conversation with his mom in the kitchen. Last he'd spoken to Amy, she'd said she quit bartending because the tips sucked.

He'd hoped it meant she was rethinking college. After seven years, she should have already gotten past the temporary gig stage. Yeah, LA was expensive, but in the beginning, the two of them had shared a place so things couldn't have been too bad.

"Is Amy still working in that bar? Where is it, Covina? Close to where the two of you used to live?"

Becca's eyes widened and she looked down at her plate.

"Ryder, I think you might have missed that Becca and I were talking about her mother."

He hadn't realized. Which could explain the look he'd gotten, but he doubted it. "Sorry."

Becca studied him a second, then turned back to his

mom. "No, she seems to love it in Alaska, even though it's colder than Montana. I don't understand that at all."

Gail chuckled. "What does an activist do?"

"She and Scott are into the politics of climate change. They write letters, make trips to Washington, DC, to talk to lobbyists and members of Congress. They also monitor the glaciers and changes in the environment."

"I had no idea Katie was interested in that sort of thing."

Ryder had been half listening and had his eyes on Becca. He saw her stiffen at his mom's comment, and figured he knew why. Shortly after her parents' divorce, Katie had met someone online. Scott had been involved with environmental issues, and within eight months, Katie had announced they were getting married and she was moving to Alaska.

Quiet, sensible Becca had flipped out. Refused to leave Blackfoot Falls. So her mom had left, and Becca had stayed with her grandparents. And for the next year, she'd rebelled in all kinds of ways that had shocked everyone.

"What about your father? Is he still working abroad?"

A trace of sadness crossed Becca's face.

Damn, his mom was batting a thousand. She must've forgotten what had brought Becca and her mom to Blackfoot Falls. It had been during her dad's second deployment that they'd moved in with Katie's parents.

"Yes, he's working somewhere in the Middle East," Becca said. "It took him a while to adjust to civilian life, but frankly, I don't see how working for a defense contractor is all that different from the military."

"For one thing, they get paid a hell of a lot more," Ryder said and caught his mom's disapproving look. Yeah, he needed to watch his language in front of the kid.

Noah's mischievous little grin confirmed he'd caught that slip.

"It's not all about money," Becca said. "He had a responsibility to his family." She bowed her head. "Sorry if I sound snippy. I do give him credit for at least trying to make something of my grandparents' place. He just wasn't cut out for ranching."

Gail put down her fork. "I'm sorry I brought it up, honey, I should've known better," she said, reaching over to pat Becca's arm. "Please forgive me."

"Nothing to forgive. I don't even know why I reacted. We talk two, three times a year. Everything's fine with us." Becca's reassuring smile eased Gail's frown and earned her a couple of points in Ryder's estimation.

Of course she still hadn't answered his question about the bar where Amy supposedly worked. But if she thought that was going to dissuade him from asking again, she was dead wrong.

After several minutes of quiet eating, Ryder said, "I didn't catch the name of that steakhouse chain you work for."

Becca finished chewing. Probably stalling while she devised another lie. "You wouldn't know it. The restaurants are only in southern California." She turned to Noah. "Everything's good, huh?"

Oh, yeah, she was holding something back. Becca had always been forthcoming. She and Amy had jabbered all the time. She might have been shy around strangers, but at the Mitchell ranch, her whole life had been an open book.

Ryder caught his mother's eye. She hadn't been this spry in a long time. He'd seen her standing at the stove, cooking up a storm, her cane nowhere in sight.

Maybe he shouldn't press Becca yet. He didn't want

to see the light go out in his mom's face because he'd chased Becca away. But before she left Blackfoot Falls, he'd find out what was going on with Amy. Becca could count on that.

Chapter Eight

Ryder poured his second cup of coffee, hoping it would wake him the hell up. He hadn't gotten to sleep until after 1:00 a.m. but that hadn't stopped his alarm clock from going off at six.

Every time he punched his pillow, determined that he wasn't going to think about the secrets Becca was holding onto, he lasted about two minutes before another unanswered question came to roost. He'd worked himself into a lather, until it had finally dawned on him that maybe the secrets had more to do with Becca than his sister.

"What's that frown for?" Gail asked, walking into the kitchen, the cane in her right hand not taking much of her weight.

"Not enough sleep," he muttered. "I mean, what's the deal with all the secrecy, huh? Has Becca told you why she came back to town? Or where Amy is? Or even if—?"

"Whoa there, mister." Gail got her usual mug from the cupboard before she faced him. "I have some questions of my own. Why are you being so ugly to Becca? What's she done to make you so mad? She's always been like one of the family, and I can tell she's a great mother even though she's on her own in a big city."

"Did she tell you that? That she's on her own, I mean? Maybe she's back because she ran out on her husband."

His mom chuckled. "Even if she had, which I seriously doubt, it wouldn't be any of our business. You should really try to get another hour of sleep."

"So you don't think she's being evasive? She's the one who dragged Amy to LA, and now she's back and doesn't know where Amy is."

His mother shook her head as she gently pushed Ryder away from the coffeepot. "You think Becca talked your sister into leaving? Honey, you don't know Amy as well as you think you do." She paused, frowning. "Actually, that's probably true."

His mom, too? Becca had made a similar comment. "What's that supposed to mean?"

"You went off to college when she was eleven."

"So? I came home every summer and holidays."

"And let's see…you spent most of that time working the ranch and mooning over Leanne, and if I remember correctly, getting into some trouble at the Watering Hole."

Ryder grunted. Guess he was never going to live that minor skirmish down. And he hadn't even started the fight. "I hung out with Amy sometimes. We talked."

"Then you should know that your sister didn't let anyone tell her what to do. Not me, not your dad and certainly not Becca. Our girl has had one foot out the door since she was ten."

He leaned against the counter, watching his mom pour cream in her coffee. Granted, Amy could be headstrong, but he knew what might've lit the fire under her.

Shortly after Becca had moved in with her grandparents—when the girls were around ten—she'd started telling Amy about the big exciting cities she'd lived in when her father had gotten transferred. Ryder had heard some of it while they were hanging around the stable, but he hadn't thought much of it then. In hindsight, it might've made Amy feel like a country bumpkin. And that sure could've helped push her out the door.

Hell, it was just kid stuff, though. He couldn't blame Becca for trying to fit in and impress a new friend with her tales. Just last night, he'd recalled how she'd dug in her heels and wouldn't leave Blackfoot Falls for Alaska. Though that might've had more to do with the new stepfather.

His mom patted him on the shoulder. "You had breakfast yet?"

"Two hours ago."

"Well, then you'd best quit lollygagging in the kitchen when you should be working." She pulled out her cast iron skillet. "I think there's a little boy coming down the hall who's gonna love my flapjacks."

"I had lumpy oatmeal from the bunkhouse, but don't worry about me."

"I'm not. Now get it in gear. You've got a ranch to run."

He sighed as dramatically as he could, taking his insulated mug with him, then paused at the door. "Last night, you mentioned something about Becca going to community college."

"The one in Kalispell," she said, nodding. "What about it?"

"How did you know?"

"How did—?" Her brows arched. "It wasn't a secret. She'd worked a part-time job during her senior year to save money for tuition."

Huh.

"Doesn't sound like a girl who was all fired up to leave town first chance she got, does it?"

Ryder grunted at her smug smile and stepped outside. He took a big sip and burned his tongue. His curse wasn't so loud it would bother his mother, but it helped.

Walking to the barn, he thought about what his mom and Becca had both said about him not knowing Amy. He had to admit he hadn't spent a lot of real, one-on-one time with her. Seven years was a big gap between siblings, and besides, she was a girl. He hadn't even been allowed to tease her when they were both kids.

Which wasn't what stuck in his craw. That Amy hadn't been coerced into leaving was a problem. Because it painted a different picture of Becca. He'd been blaming her for every wrong thing that had happened to Amy since she'd gone to LA.

Wiley's ATV came rumbling from the back shed, and Ryder welcomed the distraction.

"I'm going to check the fence line along the south pasture. Bear said something got into it last night."

"Did any of it come down?"

"I don't think so. At least not yet. I hope another doe didn't get her hooves caught," Wiley said, grimly. "You headed to Evergreen to look at those herd sires?"

"That's next week."

"Oh, right. You got a few minutes to talk about the holiday schedule then?"

Ryder took another, more cautious sip. "Whatever you decide is okay with me. You know that."

"I'm talking all the way out to Christmas. If everyone who wants time off gets it, we'll have a skeleton crew."

His thoughts scattered, Ryder nodded. He didn't know why Wiley felt compelled to run things by him. The guy had been the foreman since before Ryder had left for college. His dad had trusted Wiley to keep the ranch in top shape and so did Ryder. In fact, being able to rely on Wiley had freed Ryder up to expand their holdings.

As a result, he'd become less involved in the day-to-day operation.

He let Wiley go on describing the winter projects he'd prioritized, only half listening, his mind jumping back to things Becca or his mom had said at dinner. In what seemed like a minute, over a half an hour had gone by. Enough time to wonder if Wiley's feelings for his mom had anything to do with this wave of uncertainty. Maybe he didn't want Ryder to think he was being edged out. Hell, that never would've crossed his mind.

Just as Ryder was about to put out feelers, Wiley broke into a broad grin. The sound of little feet slapping the dirt shed some light on the matter. Ryder looked over his shoulder.

Sure enough it was Noah, wearing jeans, sneakers and a denim jacket. When the boy came to a rocking stop in front of him, he saw that he had on a sweatshirt, too. "Can we go do horse things, Uncle Ryder?"

"Horse things?"

Noah jumped, but only one time. "I finished all my pancakes and Aunt Gail said I could come outside and that there were gloves in the bunker that would fit."

"I think you mean the bunkhouse," Wiley said. "And I do believe I know where those gloves might be. How about you hop on and I'll take you to get 'em, and then you can come with me to do real cowboy stuff."

"With horses?"

"Even better," Wiley said. "Cows. Lots of 'em. You ever met a cow?"

"I met a goat once. Are cows as big as horses?"

"I'll let you be the judge. How about it?" Wiley looked to Ryder to give the okay, and when he did, Wiley slid back on the seat and tucked Noah safely in front of him before he said, "Ready?"

"Can I wear your cowboy hat?"

"We'll see about that once we catch up to the cows."

"Don't stay out too long," Ryder said.

"Wave to Uncle Ryder, Noah."

The boy did, but when the older man took off, at a very stately pace, Noah grabbed on to Wiley's worn jeans with tight fists.

Ryder trusted Wiley not to scare the kid, but he kept a watchful eye on their trip to the bunkhouse. After the motor cut off, Noah got off the ATV and immediately started hopping.

Ryder smiled. It was going to be an adventure for both of them. A couple of minutes later, the duo climbed aboard the ATV once more, with gloves that looked a few sizes too big. Then they were off.

Ryder sipped his coffee as they proceeded up the hill, then he heard the kitchen door slam behind him. Becca. She wasn't walking quite as quickly as Noah had, but close.

"Where are they going?"

He waited until she was close enough to speak without raising his voice. "Wiley's just taking him to the south pasture to look at some downed fence."

Her jaw flexed in agitation. "You should have asked me first."

She was right. As soon as he'd heard the door slam, he'd realized his mistake. He'd already seen what kind of mother Becca was—sensible, attentive, careful. Noah had excellent manners and he listened well, which wasn't something Ryder had seen a lot of in his friends' children. And most of them were being raised by stay-at-home moms. He'd hoped to have a son about Noah's age by now—not a thought he wanted to pursue at the moment.

"When will they be back?"

Ryder shook his head. “Not sure. Remember, this is ranch country. We don’t have set times for things. It all depends on what Wiley sees when he gets out to the pasture.”

The agitation was now accompanied by worry lines on her forehead. Realizing his second mistake, he moved closer to her. “Look, I shouldn’t have been so flippant. Wiley won’t keep him out there long. He wanted to show Noah some cows, and I guess we both got a little carried away. But if you’d like, I can call him right now and tell him to turn back.”

Becca shook her head, looking in the direction the ATV had traveled. “No. It’s fine. Noah should get the chance to see everything he can before we leave tomorrow.”

He would’ve thought she was taking a jab at him if he hadn’t seen the way she was staring at that trail. The annoyance and concern were gone. Her expression had turned wistful, almost as if she were jealous that she wasn’t riding out into the wild blue along with them.

“You sure you want to leave so soon? I mean, I don’t know, maybe Noah has this much fun every day back in the city, but man, he sure does seem to love being on the ranch.”

Becca’s right eyebrow rose as she turned to look at him. No, he hadn’t been exactly welcoming. Maybe it was time to get a little more creative.

“I know my mom is getting a huge kick out of you two being here, especially for the holiday.”

Becca laughed. “Getting ahead of yourself, aren’t you?”

“What? Thanksgiving is only two days away. You’ll still be here, won’t you?”

“In Blackfoot Falls, you mean?”

He smiled, nodded.

"I'm not sure."

"I figured you were on vacation."

"We are." She folded her arms across her chest in a defensive stance.

Hell, it wasn't as if he'd been baiting her. Maybe a little. "You gonna travel on Thanksgiving? Try your luck at a restaurant on the way? I already know what kind of meal Otis and Mom are gonna be fixing, and if you think last night's dinner was—"

"I've been to Thanksgiving here before," she said, sticking her hands in her jacket pockets. Her coat might be lined, but it wouldn't be warm enough for the change that was coming.

When it seemed clear that was all she was going to say, he figured he had nothing to lose by taking one more shot. He wanted her to stay. Only for his mom's sake. "You feel like getting back in the saddle? Miss Kitty would sure enjoy it."

She laughed, but when she turned to face him full on, she was shaking her head. "I don't even know if I can ride anymore."

"You learned when you were twelve. That's not something you forget."

Studying him with her head tilted slightly, she looked surprised he'd remembered. Of course he had. He and his dad had been the ones who'd taught her. "I may have learned early, but I didn't ride much. Only during the summers and holidays when you were home from school." She shrugged. "Even that petered out after you took up with Leanne and—" She blinked. "What?"

"Interesting way to put it," he said, but she still seemed puzzled. "Took up with Leanne?"

"Oh." Her gaze shifted away and she blushed slightly. "You knew what I meant."

She had a faint sprinkling of freckles across her nose. How had he not noticed that before? He wanted a closer look, which was never going to happen. To be safe, he moved as far back as he could without being obvious.

"It wasn't just that I *took up* with Leanne," he said, smiling when Becca rolled her eyes. "I seem to recall you were pretty busy yourself." He knew the exact moment she realized he was referring to her fling with rebellion.

She laughed and groaned at the same time. "Yeah, thanks for bringing that up."

"Like the time you and Amy sneaked off and hitched a ride to Kalispell to go to that concert?"

"That would be one example." She looked down, shook her head again, this time wearing a crooked smile. "That was just after I found out my mom was moving to Alaska." She scuffed her boot on the dirt. They were ankle boots, black and better suited for city streets.

"I know that was rough on you."

"I understand more now about why Scott's life seemed exciting. He was already living in Alaska, working to change things, and Mom needed something to be involved in."

"Something more important than raising her daughter?"

At his dry tone, she looked up, startled. Or maybe she'd reacted to what he'd said, not how he'd said it. He should've kept the comment to himself…

Except Becca, with her soft hazel eyes, was looking at him as if he'd hung the moon and threw in a few stars, just for her.

She blinked but didn't look away.

Something eased inside him.

Then she gave him a shy little smile that didn't do anything to help get him back on track. It might've even bucked him off a couple more feet.

"Sorry," he said gruffly. "I should've kept my opinion to myself."

"I didn't hear an opinion." Using the toe of her boot, she drew a design in the dirt. "To be fair, I think the real problem was that I didn't expect her to actually leave."

"She just up and left?"

"No. She gave me the choice to go with her or stay with my grandparents." Becca shrugged. "I admit, I wanted her to choose me over some guy she'd met on the internet."

"Well, sure." Ryder noticed the pink returning to her cheeks, so he focused on drinking his coffee.

"I didn't mean to get so maudlin. Or whiny."

"You were a kid. You had every reason to feel that way. I can see why you acted out."

"Yeah. Not very original, but it probably did me some good. I wasn't all that fond of being wild and carefree. Not really my style."

"Come on. Let me saddle up Miss Kitty. You and she both need to stretch your legs."

"So I'll be walking next to her?"

"Not the kind of stretch I was referring to."

The pink came back to her cheeks. "I honestly don't think—"

"You don't want to humiliate yourself in front of Noah, do you? You're his hero. You gave a horse a bath, remember?"

Sighing, she rolled her eyes. "Fine. But we're walking. No trotting."

Ryder laughed, glad they'd found some common ground. It didn't change what he wanted to know, but it did make it a lot more comfortable for both of them. He'd assumed a lot about her, about Amy, which was a mistake. Lots of things had happened in the intervening years. To both Amy and Becca. And to him, as well.

By the time they were both on their saddles, she was more relaxed than he'd expected. He stuck to her ground rules and walked the horses toward the pasture, figuring they'd meet up or pass Wiley and Noah at some point.

"Okay," she said, when they were just about at the top of the hill, "maybe we can canter a little. When we see Noah. But nothing fancy."

"Nothing fancy," he repeated. "Check."

"I'm not kidding. It's been years since I've done this, and I don't want to spend all night soaking in Epsom salts."

He laughed hard. It was true, though. First rides were not kind on backsides. But then, he couldn't help picturing Becca in the tub. She'd blossomed into a very attractive woman. No denying that. But to think of her in that way? Not smart. Not even for a few minutes.

"I never realized four-year-olds were so energetic," he said, slipping right into the safe zone.

"You're joking."

"'Fraid not. I pictured having babies, you know, walking them around the house, buckling them into high chairs. Then I seemed to skip a lot and moved right on to how I'd teach them to ride and rope and catch a baseball."

"Hoping for all boys, hmm?"

"No. Girls can do all those things, too."

Becca smiled briefly, then said, "I'm sorry that didn't work out for you."

He shrugged. "I've still got time. And I'm sorry it didn't work out with you and Noah's dad. Does Noah ask about him?"

Becca tensed, her hands clutching the reins tighter, back even straighter. But then she eased up just a tick. "Not yet," she said. "I know the time will come, though."

"Does he at least help financially?"

Her shoulders drooped. "Can we please not talk about this?"

Ryder couldn't help noticing the sadness that shadowed her eyes. Even her voice sounded drained. "Look, I really do want you two to stay longer," he said, "at least through Thanksgiving, so I promise, no more upsetting questions. What do you say?"

"I should've known you were trying to butter me up."

"Me? Butter you up?"

She raised both eyebrows.

"Okay. You're almost right. It's no secret my mom is loving that Noah's here, but also that you're here. I don't know what's going on with Amy, but you've been a real tonic, and I want Mom to have a nice holiday for a change."

"So do I, Ryder. Truly. It's been wonderful to see you, for Noah to be around the ranch. I've been trying to—"

Her phone rang, and she dove into her pocket for it, as if the phone would mysteriously vanish if she didn't answer it in the next second.

He tried to act as if he wasn't listening, when he was doing nothing but.

She frowned, then said, "You've got the wrong number," and hung up.

Wrong number? Her whole demeanor had changed. She bit nervously at her lower lip, her thoughts as faraway as the Rockies behind her.

Becca finally looked at him. "I was hoping it was Amy," she said, her voice barely carrying on the breeze.

Yeah, but she didn't want him to think anything was wrong.

Amy simply had other plans. That was all.

He'd promised, though. No more upsetting questions. At least for the time being.

Chapter Nine

Becca pulled up the duvet on the queen bed until it was just under Noah's chin. He'd fought so hard to stay awake, insisting he was too old for naps. But after getting up at an ungodly hour this morning, he'd helped brush Miss Kitty, relentlessly chased the poor barn cat, "helped" feed the horses and clean out the stable and had a tuna sandwich for lunch while he grilled Gail about what they were having for dinner tonight.

Becca could have used a nap herself, but instead she'd volunteered to help Gail with the pre-holiday prep. In a minute. Right now, she wanted to watch her darling boy sleep, his long dark lashes casting tiny shadows high on his cheeks. She loved him so much it hurt.

Of course, Amy loved him, too, and for four years, Becca had grappled with the fact that Amy's life could turn around and that she'd beg to have her son back.

Becca wished she knew where Amy was. She'd begun thinking the worst, but yesterday's call from Derek had revived her hope that Amy had gotten away.

Although why she hadn't contacted Becca still bothered her. Derek had been obviously high when he'd threatened her, which was extremely unusual. Dealing was big business for him so he liked to keep a clear head.

If he was using, things had probably gone badly with his Mexican supplier.

That was good news for Becca. He'd sounded too messed up to actually be a threat.

She blew out a breath. She still wasn't sure what she would do when she did hear from her friend. Amy had a long road to recovery ahead of her. Assuming she wanted to get clean. Either way, she'd have to move out of LA, go someplace where Derek wouldn't find her.

Would she expect Becca to quit her job and follow with Noah? And if Amy didn't call, would Becca and Noah have to leave LA anyway? If Derek still proved to be a threat, then of course…

A shudder passed through her. Why hadn't she considered that possibility before now? She might have if she wasn't so tired and on edge. More likely it was because she hadn't wanted to face facts. There were so many distractions here, not the least of which was the changeable Ryder.

There was also the chance that Amy might decide to come back home. Which would turn Becca's life upside down.

Of course she'd want Noah with her. And of course, Gail and Ryder would hate Becca for not having told them the truth. She wouldn't even blame them. The Mitchells were good people. She almost wished she hadn't agreed to stay through Thanksgiving. How could her conscience allow her to leave without telling them about Noah, and possibly losing him forever?

Becca stood when her eyes misted, leaned over and kissed her son's cheek. "You'll always be the son of my heart," she whispered. "No matter what."

Then she left the bedroom, determined not to let even one tear fall. It helped that Gail was scrambling about the kitchen, opening cupboards and pulling out pots and dishes. Her cane leaned against the wall a good seven feet away. "Gail?"

She looked up, baking pan still in her hand. "Is he sleeping?"

"Down for the count. He's had such a busy day. And it looks like you have, too. I hope all this fuss isn't on our account."

"I've missed this. We haven't had a real Thanksgiving in too long. Wait till you try Otis's cornbread stuffing."

"Now, I seem to remember a certain secret-recipe mashed potatoes dish that I liked so much I had to skip pie until the next day."

Gail's eyes gleamed. "Well, try to save some room, because I'm not only making the mash, I'm also making my famous pumpkin pie, with the flakiest crust in Montana."

Grinning, Becca, who'd left the bedroom with her cell phone in hand, went to put it in the back pocket of her jeans. Only it didn't slide in nearly as easily as it should have. "Oh, God. No pie for me. Or mashed potatoes. How long have we been here, two and a half days? And my jeans are already too tight. How is that even possible?"

Laughing, Gail put the pan on the counter. "Don't be silly, you look wonderful," she said as she looked past her. "I need the big casserole dish from the top shelf and for someone to pick something up for me in town."

Turning her head, Becca jumped at how close Ryder was standing. As he checked out her rear end…

The burn started up her neck, then spread into her cheeks and ears.

He entered the kitchen, giving her an impertinent wink as he passed, and retrieved the dish for his mother. "I sure hope you don't expect me to go to the Food Mart. It'll be a zoo."

"No. I don't."

The back door opened and Wiley entered, carrying a big box of groceries. From the weight of it, Becca imagined there was a hefty turkey inside.

"Otis asked me to bring the things you asked for," Wiley said. "And to lend a hand."

Not far behind him, Otis pushed in through the door like a man on a mission. "I never said you should lend a hand. I know better. You don't belong in a kitchen. You hear me, Gail? He's a menace. He can burn boiling water. Can't scramble an egg to save his life."

"Oh, for Pete's sake." Wiley set the box down on the counter where Gail directed him. "Quit exaggerating, you old coot."

"Do I tell you how to run this ranch? No, I don't," Otis said, waving a wooden spoon. "And you, buster, leave the cooking to those of us who know what we're doing."

"Who said I was gonna cook? I can fetch and carry so Gail doesn't have to. I can set a table." Wiley turned to Gail with a smile that could melt butter. "I can wash dishes and do whatever needs doing. Don't listen to Otis. He's gone funny in the head."

"Stop fussing," Gail said, looking from one man to the other, then lingering briefly on Wiley. "Both of you. Just stand there and be quiet while I talk to Ryder for a minute."

Becca's gaze shifted to Ryder. Was she imagining things or was Wiley flirting with Gail?

Ryder held her gaze just long enough to tell her she hadn't imagined it. Then he smiled at his mother.

"I need you to go to the bakery," Gail said. "Kylie will have something boxed and ready for you."

Becca groaned. "Bakery? Oh, no. Maybe I should go to Abe's Variety and buy a bigger pair of jeans."

Ryder laughed, then quickly cleared his throat. "Want to come with me?"

Then it was Wiley exchanging an am-I-imaging-things look with Otis.

"I was kidding," she said. "Sort of. Noah's napping, and I have no idea what time he'll get up. Besides, I'm going to help your mother."

"Got that covered," Wiley said, fixing the collar of his plaid flannel shirt.

"See?" Ryder pulled out his keys. "She's got all the help she needs."

"But Noah..."

"Nonsense," Gail said. "I'm perfectly capable of taking care of him until you get back. Besides, I can't think with all of you in my kitchen. Now go, you two, and don't hurry back."

Ryder plucked his denim jacket from the rack by the door and then tossed the puffy one to Becca. As she followed him, she heard Otis and Wiley start in again.

"I CAN'T BELIEVE how comfortable your truck is." Becca ran her hand over the creamy leather of the passenger seat. "I feel like I'm riding in a limo."

Smiling, Ryder kept his eyes on the road as they turned onto the highway. "That compact you're driving, isn't it the same car you had when you left?"

"Yep. It's got over two hundred thousand miles on it—held together with duct tape and prayers—but it got us here in one piece. I just hope it gets us back, too."

Ryder slid her a look. "Doesn't sound like you're joking."

"I'm not. Okay, I am," she added quickly. "I hope you know I wouldn't do anything to endanger Noah." She winced about the same time Ryder gave her a funny look.

Well, of course he did. It was a stupid thing for her to say, since he had no idea Noah was his nephew. To reboot the conversation, she said the next thing that popped into her head. "I ride the bus to work most days."

"How long does it take you?"

"By bus, forty minutes each way."

"What?"

"That's really not bad considering how spread out the city is. Plus I save a ton on gas. And I don't have to pay for parking."

"Ah, that's right. Those parking fees are steep, especially in the downtown area."

"You've been there?"

Ryder nodded. "I guess Amy didn't mention it."

"No, she didn't." That was weird. Why hadn't she said anything? Unless she'd been high and had forgotten. "When?"

"About a year ago."

Becca's brain was racing a hundred miles a minute, and so was her pulse. She took a quiet moment to settle her nerves, telling herself that Ryder would've mentioned his visit before now if it had revealed anything Becca should worry about. The possibility that he was baiting her couldn't be ignored either.

"You didn't actually see her, did you?" she asked, realizing she might be overreacting. "Because it's just so weird that she didn't say anything to me."

"Well, I didn't make the trip specifically to see her. We still had her phone number back then. I had business in Ventura and I was hoping she had a little time for me. Can't say I was surprised that she didn't."

"Oh." Becca turned to look out her window, and after several minutes of silence, he turned on the radio. To a country music station.

"What's that smile for?" he asked.

"Remember when you taught Amy and me to line dance?"

Ryder groaned. "Yeah, thanks for bringing that up. We're even now."

"No. Wait," she said, laughing at his pained expression. "I don't know what you're thinking of, but we had a blast." When all he did was shake his head in disgust, she laughed harder. "Come on, don't you remember?"

"Yeah, you guys might've had fun but I got razzed by half the football team."

"When? How?" She gave his arm a light shove when he wouldn't respond. "Come on, tell me."

"We were outside, behind the barn. You and Amy must've been about ten, and I was a senior. I bet you can fill in the rest."

Becca bet she could have, too, if she wasn't having the strangest reaction to touching him. For goodness' sake, it was just an arm. That she was still touching. For no reason. None at all.

She snatched her hand back.

Ryder gave her a look he'd never given her before. His eyes had darkened to a midnight blue and his nostrils flared ever so slightly. It was kind of sexy.

A surge of warmth took her by surprise. She felt the usual blush stinging her cheeks, a curse to fair skin and nothing she had any control over. The heat continued to spread, not just up her neck but down to her chest and lower.

Much lower.

She shifted against the seat belt. Squirming didn't help one bit.

Luckily, they'd just reached the town limits, slowing down as they passed The Boarding House Inn and continuing on Main Street. There were quite a few people roaming the sidewalks and lots of cars were parked in front of the diner. Some folks were congregating outside the bakery, and the two bars seemed to be hopping as well.

A battered truck pulled out just in time for Ryder to take the spot right across from Abe's Variety. She'd only been joking about buying new jeans. Now, all she could think about was Abe's wide selection of old-fashioned candies.

"What?" Ryder said, just as he opened his door.

"I didn't say anything."

"You snorted."

Bristling, she opened her door. "I don't snort."

"Of course not," he said.

They met on the sidewalk, his teasing little smile helping her relax. She was enjoying this side of Ryder, the one she'd known as a girl. "Mind if we meander a bit?" she asked. "I haven't seen much of the town since I got here."

"Let's go." He put his hand on the small of her back, which probably meant nothing at all, but it gave her a tingling sensation that was hard to ignore.

A couple leaving the Watering Hole was too busy laughing to realize they were hogging the sidewalk. Ryder's hand slipped away, but before Becca's silly disappointment took a firm hold, he moved it to her waist and pulled her closer to him.

Good Lord, she hoped he didn't notice her little shiver. His move was strictly practical, meant to avoid running into the couple, but tell that to her body. The tingling was starting to be a problem. Then his hand did fall away as they were passing the bar. Country music spilled out as a cowboy pushed through the door.

"I'm glad to know that's still up and running," Becca

said. "I assume Sadie still owns it. Last time I saw her was at my grandfather's funeral, but we didn't really speak. She was a good friend to Grams."

"If you want, we can stop in for a beer later," Ryder said. "No guarantee Sadie will be there, though. She still owns it, but now that she's also the mayor, her schedule's all over the place."

"Sadie's the mayor?"

"Yep. Damn good one, too."

They walked past the bank and the *Salina Gazette* office, then Becca stopped. "This used to be a bar, but it wasn't called the Full Moon, was it?"

"Nope. I don't remember the old name. The place had been closed for over ten years before Mallory bought it. She has live music on the weekends, pool tables in the back. And a mechanical bull that's pretty popular."

She frowned at the sly glint in his eyes. "Not a chance."

"I didn't say anything."

"I still can't believe you got me on a horse."

"It was fun," he said, nudging her with his elbow. "Admit it."

"I was just happy not to embarrass myself."

"You did great," he said, pausing at the bottleneck in front of the bakery. "Either we wait in line or we could go check out that mechanical bull."

"Go right ahead. I'll wait."

Ryder laughed.

"The Cake Whisperer is such a great name. I saw it from the Food Mart and didn't dare come near it. Although now that I see they serve all kinds of coffee…"

"It's crazy in there with everyone picking up their orders," he said, looking over people's heads. "We can come back another day for coffee."

Another day?

Becca wished she understood him. She liked the old Ryder, who'd taught her to ride and to line dance. Who'd never gotten impatient no matter how many questions she'd asked. And that wink in the kitchen? She got a little squishy just thinking about it. But five minutes from now would he again be that unrecognizable man with contempt in his eyes?

Actually, it was safer to believe his change in attitude was a ploy to coax her into spilling everything she knew about Amy. And then, too, he'd admitted he wanted her and Noah to stay for Gail. So of course he'd tread lightly.

When it was their turn, Ryder went in to get his mom's order while she stayed outside hoping no one stopped to chat her up. Thankfully, he wasn't long.

The white box wasn't very big. "Do you know what's in there?" she asked as he turned them around and started walking again.

"Nope. Want a peek?"

She shook her head. "I hope it isn't something special for Noah, after he rudely announced he didn't like pumpkin pie."

"I wouldn't bet against it."

"He's getting spoiled. Before you know it, he'll be snapping his fingers."

Ryder grinned. "You've done a great job with him. He's not going to suddenly become a brat."

"I hope not. Anyway, it's just for one more day."

He nodded at a cowboy who stepped out of the Full Moon, but Ryder had lost the smile, clearly displeased with the small reminder she'd thrown in. Although it honestly hadn't been intentional.

When they got to his truck, he stashed the box on the back seat. Then he took her arm and led her into the Watering Hole.

Chapter Ten

The place was crowded but they found a table in the corner. Just as he'd suspected, Sadie wasn't around. Nikki was pouring, and when Ryder noticed they were a waitress short, he left Becca at the table and went to the bar to order two beers.

There were a number of what he assumed were dude ranch guests, given their flirty outfits, and as always, a lot of cowboys. Tomorrow, Marge's Diner would cook up a big Thanksgiving dinner for all the strays that didn't have family in town. But tonight was popular for picking up dates.

He turned back to check on Becca, who was looking toward the poolroom. Her hair seemed darker in here. Outside, the sun picked up the coppery highlights. She looked especially pretty with her hair down and tumbling off her shoulders.

"I haven't seen you in here before."

Ryder started when he noticed the woman standing so close to him. Sundance guest. Had to be. "I don't come in much," he said, giving her a polite half smile.

"Pity," she said, boldly sizing him up. "Not that I don't like these young cowboys, but honestly, what they don't know is…kind of staggering."

Nikki brought the two beers. He'd already laid down

enough to cover them both plus a decent tip, so he made his escape without much difficulty. The blonde's sigh followed him a couple of steps.

Becca was looking just past him, at least until he was almost at the table. Once he'd settled and they'd each taken a sip, she glanced back at the bar. "Do you mind if I ask how long you've been divorced?"

"Three years now. About."

She nodded, her attention fully on him as she took another swig of beer. "I hope Noah's not being any trouble for Gail."

"I doubt it. He seemed right at home." He exchanged nods with a guy from the Circle K as the man passed their table. "What you said about him being spoiled has got me thinking. I can tell you're not big on giving in to his every whim, and you're right not to. I'll say something to Wiley and Mom about cooling it, and I'll do the same myself. I don't want you having a problem with him later."

"Thank you, Ryder. But please don't." She almost touched his hand but pulled back at the last moment. "I'd hate for them to feel uncomfortable."

"I think they'd want it pointed out, just like I did. He's a great kid, it's easy to get carried away with him."

"I really do try to give him a good foundation, and I believe that setting boundaries is my job. It makes life a lot more manageable for him, and for whoever's caring for him. He'll bounce back soon enough."

"That was my folks' approach, too, but I'm pretty sure by the time Amy came around, they were too tired to fuss much. She got away with way more than I did."

"Ah, the Ballad of Every Older Sibling. I'm surprised that isn't on the jukebox."

"Very amusing. Especially for an only child." He

smiled at her, glad that for the first time, the mention of Amy hadn't spun Becca into a funk.

"I know enough." She sipped again and grimaced slightly. "I don't even like beer that much, but I'm so thirsty."

"I'd be happy to get you a glass of water."

"Thanks, but I can get it," she said, glancing at the bar. "Later, if I still want some."

"You sure? Because I don't mind." For someone who didn't care for beer, she'd downed half a mug already.

"Nope. I'm good." She strained for a look into the back where the pool tables were crowded with players and spectators. "I'm surprised I don't recognize more people. There's a guy wearing a brown shirt who I think I went to school with. Kevin something or other. He's about the right age."

Ryder stopped mid-sip and studied her profile. It hadn't occurred to him she might be interested in looking up guys she knew from high school. He didn't know what bothered him more, that she could be on the prowl or that he cared. A little too much.

She leaned farther back, trying for a better look. The arch made her breasts thrust from the front of her open jacket. Her thick sweater disguised nothing.

Damn, it was hard not to look.

She came forward with an abruptness that caused him to spill some of his beer. Luckily, he'd pulled back his gaze in time.

"It's warm in here, isn't it?" She took another hearty sip, then drew her shoulders back and struggled out of her jacket.

Cosmic justice was a bitch. He kept his eyes on his mug until she was finished.

"Aren't you warm?" she asked.

Shaking his head, he wondered at the pink in her cheeks. She blushed easily, but he hadn't said anything to embarrass her. And he doubted she'd seen him looking for those few seconds. But it was possible…

"Are you seeing anyone?" she asked.

"Me? Nope."

"I mean, since you mentioned you figured you would've had kids of your own by now, I just assumed… There certainly are a lot of pretty women in town. I would have thought you'd have your pick."

"Ah, you haven't heard about the Sundance."

"The McAllisters' place? Sure I have."

"Not just a ranch anymore. They run a dude ranch. Most of the women you see here are staying there on vacation. They're from places like Los Angeles and Chicago. City women out for a fling."

"Well, that must be nice. At least you have plenty of opportunities to get laid." In a split second, her cheeks went from pink to red. "Oh, my God." She lifted a hand to cover her mouth. "I just said that out loud…"

He eyed her almost-empty mug and tried to keep a straight face. "You don't drink much, do you?"

"Oh, God. No. I don't. I'm sorry. I really don't. Maybe three beers in my whole life. If something special happens, I might have a glass of wine. I really am sorry. That was so rude of me."

"You're fine," he said, then gave in to a grin. "It was a very astute observation." He could tell she'd told him the truth. She must not get out much, even though she was just as pretty and around the same age as the woman who'd flirted with him. "When was the last time you went out on a date?"

"What?" She blinked. "Where did that come from?"

"I was thinking about how you work full time, then have to run home to Noah—"

"I don't consider him an inconvenience."

"Of course not, and I didn't say that he was."

She sighed. "Five years."

Ryder frowned. "Five years," he repeated, then it struck him. "Five years since you've been on a date?"

"So?" she murmured, shrugging. "It's not a big deal."

He tried to keep his reaction to a minimum. Becca truly was young. Twenty-five, like Amy. But she shouldered a much bigger load. She'd been mostly responsible as a girl, and she still was. Needed to be, what with being a single mother in a city like LA. Naturally, she didn't have time for bars and dates and boyfriends.

"Oh, heck, I've already humiliated myself, and I've been dying to know, so I'm just going to ask," she said, leaning in so her elbows were on either side of her mug. "Is something going on between Wiley and your mom?"

He wasn't sure what to say, so he stalled by draining his beer.

"I'm sorry. That was way too nosy. It's none of my business."

He put his empty mug down. "No, that was all me. I think Wiley's got a thing for her, but I don't know if Mom's noticed."

"Would that bother you?"

"To be honest, I'm not a hundred-percent sure."

"It has to be kind of weird, since you've known him forever. But it's also kind of sweet, too. I mean, you can tell he really does care about her."

"He does. I know that." Ryder realized there really wasn't anything to think about. "You know what, at the end of the day, if he makes her happy, I'm happy."

Becca smiled. A big smile that seemed to light up the room. “You’re a good son.”

He raised his mug. “Lousy husband, though.”

Becca frowned.

Hell, he had no earthly idea why he’d said that. Other than he’d been thinking about marriage and kids lately. “Can I get you some water?”

Brows furrowed, she glared at him. “Why did you say that?”

“I was just wondering that myself. Be right back.” He wasn’t getting into that discussion. He reached the bar at the same time Sadie walked in.

She glanced around, then sidled up next to him. “I’m surprised to see you here. I heard you’ve been traveling a lot and buying up all kinds of property.”

“Holiday week,” he said, shrugging. “Business is slow. With the exception of bars, apparently.”

Sadie laughed. “Booze waits for every man and never goes out of style.”

“I’ve got someone with me who’d like to say hello.” He inclined his head in Becca’s direction, then ordered a beer and water from Nikki.

“Is that Becca?” Sadie asked, squinting. “Shirley’s granddaughter? My God, she’s all grown up. And real pretty. You’re trading up, son. Good for you.”

Laughing, Ryder watched Sadie approach the table. He’d just laid down some money when Nikki returned with the drinks. “Let me buy Sadie one, too.”

“She won’t want it,” Nikki said, “but I’ll tell her you offered.”

Another Sundance guest—hell, you could spot them a mile away—walked up just as he turned for the table. “Excuse me,” he said, sidestepping the brunette.

"Where are you going?" She was tall, leggy—"What's your hurry, cowboy?"—and too forward for his taste.

He almost didn't respond, then said, "Gotta get back to my date."

When he made it to the table, Sadie and Becca were laughing about something. It took all of three seconds to figure out they'd been watching him and the brunette.

"Jesus, these women are like land mines," he muttered as he set the mug and glass in front of Becca, who couldn't stop laughing. A smile came automatically when he realized living in the city hadn't changed her, and he was awfully glad for that.

"You don't come in often enough," Sadie said. "They're tired of the same bunch of cowboys. You're fresh meat."

Ryder shook his head, then looked at Becca. "Drink your water."

"Who's the beer for?"

"You. I'm driving."

"Sadie, he's trying to get me drunk. Isn't there a law against that?" She took a quick sip of the drink still in her hand and looked up, eyes wide. "Oh, I understand you're the mayor now."

Sadie narrowed her gaze at Becca, then swung a look at Ryder. "Are you? Is she…?"

"That's her first beer." He nodded at the mug that was still a quarter of the way full, and Sadie chuckled.

"I'm not sure she needs the second one," she said quietly, and Ryder felt a prick of shame. "I wish I could stay and chat but I've got something going on down the street. Just came in to look for my new reading glasses. Becca, give me a buzz after Thanksgiving and let's have a cup of coffee, huh?"

"Sure. At The Cake Whisperer?"

"You got it."

"See you, Mayor." Ryder watched her shake her head as she walked away. "She doesn't like being called that," he explained to Becca, but she was busy staring at her watch.

He really wasn't trying to get her drunk. But he did like seeing her loose and relaxed. Not being pummeled with questions and accusations probably helped, he thought wryly.

She finally looked up from her watch. "Oh, gosh, we'd better get going. Noah must be awake by now. He better not be giving your mom a fit." She stood and he couldn't help but notice the slight wobble.

"I think we need to get something in your stomach first."

Becca's eyes widened. "Do you think Marge still has cinnamon rolls?"

"Let's find out."

At most she could only be slightly tipsy, but he put his arm around her waist just to be on the safe side as they left the bar and crossed over to the diner. Sadly, the rolls were all sold out. Becca looked heartbroken, especially since there were no tables available.

Back outside, she turned toward his truck, but he slowed her down. "The steakhouse has pretty good food."

"So does your mom. Seriously. She's always been a great cook, and I don't get to eat like I used to anymore." She smiled up at him, evidently not minding that he'd put his arm around her again.

It wasn't smart. Standing this close together. His hand resting on the curve of her hip. Her sweet scent drifting up to tease him.

"Yes, but we're closer to the steakhouse," he said, his

voice disturbingly hoarse. "I'm sure they have a table for two waiting just for us."

Jesus, this was Becca. What was wrong with him?

After he'd taken too long to gather his wits and lower his arm, Becca wouldn't let him move. She slipped her arm through his while studying him closely. Noting a hint of suspicion in her expression, he braced himself.

"You're stalling because you don't want Noah or Gail to see me drunk."

"On one beer?" A lock of hair tangled with her lashes, and he tucked it behind her ear. "You're not drunk."

"I know," she said, very deliberately. Then her lips lifted into another pretty smile. "Did you know I had a crush on you when I was twelve?"

"Um—" Evidently, Amy hadn't been teasing back then.

"Yep, I used to fantasize about—"

"Okay." Ryder cut her off. "You might be drunk after all. Come on. We're getting you fed. Now."

"But Noah—"

"Will be just fine. I'll call and let them know we'll be home in a while." He pulled out his cell phone, then moved Becca a little closer to the curb as he hit speed dial. "Hey, Mom. Would you mind feeding Noah his supper?"

After an enthusiastic yes from his mother, and verification that they made it to the bakery in time, Ryder said, "Oh, and Mom, don't bother to wait up." He winked at Becca. "We're on a date."

Chapter Eleven

An hour and a half later, Becca yawned and snuggled back into the comfort of Ryder's bucket seat. "I ate too much. Again."

"It's good practice for tomorrow night."

"You're supposed to be sympathetic."

"Believe me, I am. I should've skipped the apple pie a la mode."

"Which part?"

"The a la mode."

"That's what I thought." She peered into the darkness around them. "Where are we?"

"Ten minutes from home."

Not her home. She was getting far too comfortable with this version of Ryder. She needed to go to her grandparents' place, see if it was in shape for her and Noah to move over there while she figured out what her next step should be. "I can't believe you told your mother we were on a date."

"She knew I was joking around. Besides, it felt like a date, didn't it?"

"I wouldn't know."

"Take my word for it. We talked. We ate. We laughed. I paid."

She straightened. "Only because you shoved my money back at me."

His hand covered hers where it rested on her thigh. "I'm kidding. I was happy to take you out. In fact, if I remember correctly, I forced you into it."

"Don't remind me of my drunken behavior. So embarrassing."

"For what it's worth, I had no idea about your childhood crush."

Becca groaned. "Please don't make fun of me. I told you, I was twelve."

He smiled at her, the oncoming headlights from a big semi lighting up his face. "I wish I had known."

"You were nineteen. You would have laughed your butt off."

"If I had been seventeen? Definitely. Nineteen? I was much too mature for that."

"You're so full of it." She had a strong feeling he'd known all along, but he was trying to be nice.

He squeezed her hand before he pulled away.

Sighing, Becca made herself more comfortable as she cautioned her thoughts once again. It hadn't been a date, it never would be a date, and this whatever-it-was was simply the calm before the storm, so she might as well get over her ridiculousness.

Yes, it had been a lovely thing to pretend for a few hours that Ryder actually liked her, might even be attracted to her.

She had to admit, as much as it was inadvisable, she was attracted to him. His eyes, his smile, the scruff on his jaw. Even the way his earthy, clean scent made something inside her go a little cockeyed. But none of it was real. Except that he'd made an effort.

"Thank you," she said. "For the outing and for the

horseback ride yesterday." She turned to face his profile. "For being so kind to Noah, and for not blaming me…"

He didn't look at her or say a word. But the hand that had been covering hers moments ago tightened on the wheel.

That was a nice hit of reality she'd do well to remember.

"Maybe Amy will call tomorrow. For Thanksgiving," he said, the teasing in his tone completely gone.

"I hope so. I really do." Coincidentally, her cell phone rang and she pulled it out, her hopes sky high, but the call was from the Mitchells' landline. Noah? "Hello?"

"Mommy? Where are you? I had dinner and you weren't here. I miss you."

"I miss you too, sweetie. We're almost there. I'll be back in time for your bath and a bedtime story."

"No bath!"

"Yes, bath. You were playing hard all day. Now all you have to do is decide which story you want tonight."

"*Goodnight Moon*!"

"Well, that was quick. I'll let you read it with me, how's that?"

"Okay, Mommy." He disconnected, not even knowing his call was just what she'd needed. She could always count on Noah to lift her spirits.

The phone buzzed again, and she knew without looking it was him again. "What did you forget?" she asked.

"Lance said tomorrow I could have a cow pie. He said it's way better than pumpkin."

She'd met Lance, and she wasn't surprised. "I think Lance was teasing you, sweetie. A cow pie isn't something yummy."

"It's not?"

"No. I'll have Lance try one to prove it to you. Now, did you thank Aunt Gail for dinner?"

"Yes. And I took my plate into the kitchen."

"That's my good boy. Oh, we've just turned onto the road to the ranch. I'll see you in a few minutes."

They disconnected again.

"That damn Lance," Ryder said. "He doesn't have the sense God gave a flea. He's always playing practical jokes. I ended up landing on my ass in the dirt because of him."

She couldn't help a laugh. "Not even the boss is exempt? He does need a lesson in manners."

"Pulling something over on me is one thing, but messing with Noah? Maybe docking his pay is the only thing that'll get through his thick head."

"You should give Gail a crack at him."

Ryder barked out a laugh, so loud that it actually startled her. "You're right," he said as he pulled into the parking space closest to the house. "Or you. Nothing like an angry mama defending her cub." He put the truck in Park and turned off the engine. "Well, I guess this is the end of our date, and you know what happens next, right?"

"Um." She wished she could see his face better. "You're joking."

"I just asked a simple question," he said, leaning a little toward her and out of the shadows.

She had no business moistening her lips, not when he was staring at her like that. It was just nerves, but he wouldn't see it that way. Oh, boy, he didn't look as if he'd been joking at all.

Her heart was beating a mile a minute, and she had no idea what to do. Move in? Run for the hills? Laugh and say something funny?

A loud knock on Ryder's window made her gasp. He jerked back, then saw it was Bear, looking dead serious. Ryder let down his window. "What?"

"Boss, the back pasture water main broke and it's making a hell of a mess. Wiley's got everyone moving the cattle but we gotta do something about that pipe."

"I'll get my gear and be right out."

Bear nodded, his hat and clothes covered with a wet slicker, and he hopped onto a nearby ATV.

Ryder turned to Becca. "You mind taking in the box?"

She shook her head. "Go. Good luck."

He dashed out without another word, and she watched him run to the shed where they kept most of the ATVs and larger equipment.

It was bitterly cold out, and she knew he'd be soaked to the bone before long. And here she was, sitting in his warm truck, shamefully obsessing on whether he had actually intended to kiss her.

BECCA SAT AT the dining room table. It hadn't been set yet, as it was only noon and Thanksgiving dinner wasn't going to be served until five. She wasn't idle, though. She'd set up Noah with crayons and paper on the floor in the living room, where she could see him, while he made the decorations. She'd taken the precaution of putting a beige tarp underneath him. Everything seemed to be going along smoothly...his monologue to the turkey he was coloring had been running for approximately fifteen minutes.

She was polishing the last of the silver, a beautiful set that went with Gail's lovely Lenox bone china, which hadn't been used for a number of years.

Hearing the door to the mudroom open, she dropped the ladle and turned, leaning to the side so she could see into the kitchen.

Ryder was standing at the threshold. He looked as if he'd been through a car wash. Eyes red, dripping wet, the stubble darkening his jaw making him look sexy. Poor guy had worked all night and here she had her mind on sex. No. She thought he looked sexy. That was different.

She scooted her chair back so she didn't have to keep leaning to see.

"Well, you've certainly had yourself a time," Gail said, coming out of the pantry. "Is it fixed?"

He nodded, then glanced toward the stove.

"The coffee is fresh, and I can whip up some breakfast, if you'd like."

He shook his head, and even though he'd taken off his slicker, hat and coat, he still looked like a wet rat.

He gave his mom an exhausted smile. "Just coffee, thanks. I'd get it myself but I don't want to drip all over the floor."

"No, we don't want that," Gail said, getting a mug out of the upper cabinet. "I'm thankful you're in one piece, that the water main isn't a geyser costing you a fortune, and that you're home early enough to take a nice hot shower, then get a nap so you'll be able to enjoy dinner."

"I admit, I do need a shower. I don't know about a nap. Give me a half hour and I can help in here."

"Oh? You think Becca and I can't handle a Thanksgiving dinner?"

Becca stifled a grin.

"Fine. I'll go shower, then sleep. But I'm setting the alarm."

Gail passed him a mug of coffee and squeezed his shoulder. "You do that, sweetheart. I really want you to be able to enjoy dinner with the rest of us."

She hurried back to the stove, pausing to put her cane in the corner where it wouldn't be in the way. Becca had only seen her use the cane once today, and that was just while she'd mashed the potatoes in the pot on the stove.

Ryder looked past Becca to the living room floor. "I see you've put Noah to work."

"I'm making all the dec'rations." Noah frowned. "Do you really have to take a nap?"

"I think my mom knows what's best, just like your mom does. From what I can see, those are mighty nice-looking decorations. They're going to make Thanksgiving the best ever."

Noah grinned so hard he looked like he might pop.

Becca turned to find Ryder looking her way.

"Polishing the silver?" he asked.

"Traditions are important. You know that."

His smile was a little bigger for her, but he was weaving a bit in his big rubber boots.

"Go."

"What time is dinner?" he asked.

"Not until five," Gail said. "Or whenever you wake up."

One final nod and he backed up into the mudroom with his coffee.

"I put clean towels in the bin," Gail called out. She picked up a wooden spoon and just stood there, staring at the sink for a minute. "How's Wiley? Is he still coming for dinner or is he too tuckered out?"

"As far as I know, he'll be here." Ryder appeared again, this time somewhat drier and without the rubber boots. He looked at Becca and they shared a brief smile. "So is Otis."

"I know," Gail replied and got busy stirring a pot. Thankfully. So she didn't see Becca biting her lip. If Ryder made her laugh, she was going to clobber him. "He's bringing over his cornbread dressing in a little bit."

"Well, I think I can make it to my room without doing

any damage. You got enough coffee for me to take a refill with me?"

"All that caffeine? You'll never get to sleep."

"I doubt that." He'd entered the kitchen and Gail met him partway with the carafe.

He didn't have to go through the dining room to get to the stairs, but he did anyway, making Becca blush. For no reason. He hadn't brushed her or said anything. It was all because of last night. And they hadn't even kissed. It was highly unlikely that was what he'd had in mind anyway, she'd decided.

Gail came over to the table and sat next to her. "It looks like you two are still getting along. I'm glad."

"He's been very considerate. I appreciate it. He certainly doesn't have to be. Neither do you."

Gail's hand closed over Becca's. "I know you've been a good friend to Amy, no matter what she's gotten into that head of hers. And the way you love Noah? That's something to celebrate even if it wasn't Thanksgiving."

Becca's heart hurt. She didn't want to see this woman suffer, but Becca couldn't drag Amy back if she didn't want to come. There was very little Becca could do…

Except give Gail the grandson she so desperately wanted.

"You weren't around, so you wouldn't know." Gail glanced in the direction of the stairs. "Ryder's divorce from Leanne wasn't anyone's fault. They simply didn't fit. It happens to a lot of folks, and I was sorry to see Ryder go through the pain of it, but splitting up was the right thing to do. He needs a wife who'll understand what this ranch means to him. How hard he works."

"He does," Becca agreed. "It's a shame he doesn't already have kids of his own, though. I know how much he wants them."

Gail's surprise was evident in her face and her posture. "How did you know?"

"He mentioned it." She caught a strange glimmer in Gail's eyes and hastened to add, "In passing, that's all. He's so good with Noah, it's easy to see that he'd be great with his own brood."

"He normally doesn't like to talk about that. Even with me. He just tells me it'll happen if it's supposed to."

Becca felt bad about bringing it up.

Gail patted her hand. "Don't you fret. I won't mention anything to him. I'm really pleased that he felt he could open up to you."

"Thank you. I don't want to do anything that would threaten this truce we have."

"That's what you're calling it?" Gail's grin made her eyes sparkle.

Lord, Becca hoped she wasn't matchmaking. It was bad enough that Becca had stayed up too late thinking about that almost kiss.

Despite the blush creeping into her cheeks, she purposely rolled her eyes and picked up the cloth and the ladle.

Gail didn't press her, but when her gaze hit on Becca's cell phone, lying right there on the table, her light dimmed. "I wonder if Amy will call tonight. Wouldn't that be wonderful?"

"It would be perfect," Becca said, meaning it.

"What about your mother? Did you speak with her today?"

"I left her a message. We often communicate that way these days. Where she lives is fine, but out in the field, the cell service is unreliable. I expect I'll hear from her before too long."

"I hope Noah will be awake to wish his grandma a happy Turkey Day."

The only thought that came to Becca was that he'd already done that, and now he was drawing the *dec'rations* for her Thanksgiving holiday.

Chapter Twelve

Dinner was a big hit—the food, the conversation, the laughter, all of it. Noah's wide-eyed wonder at the size of the turkey and how much food was on the table at one time, Wiley's affection for Gail evident in every word and gesture…and the calm and warm presence of Ryder who sat at Becca's side made the meal perfect. Even Otis had left his grumpiness outside and basked in the compliments to his cornbread dressing.

Becca could have done without stuffing herself so much. She'd secretly unbuttoned the top of her jeans halfway through the meal.

Gail, who'd been in such high spirits all evening, looked over at the counter, where the old landline phone still sat. The hint of sadness dulling her eyes told Becca exactly what Gail was thinking.

"You all right?" Wiley asked.

Gail nodded. "I thought she'd have called by now."

"It's still early in LA," Becca said, even though she was reaching. "She might have forgotten the time difference."

Gail gave her a look that didn't hold much hope, but then she pulled out a smile. "Becca and I will get the desserts ready if you gents will clear the table. I've already put on some coffee and Noah can have a glass of milk."

"No pumpkin pie," Noah said, accompanied by an emphatic fist on the table.

"Noah, that's not nice," Becca said. "Aunt Gail went to a lot of trouble to make us this wonderful meal. If you don't care for something, you say 'no, thank you,' and that's it."

"But—"

"That's it."

His lower lip went out, although his pout wasn't as effective with his little gravy mustache. Becca dabbed at it with her napkin before she got up.

She was on her way to the kitchen with a few plates when she heard Gail say, "Later, I'll need someone to bring the Christmas boxes down from the attic."

It got so quiet that Becca glanced back.

All three men were staring at Gail.

"What? It's tradition. I always start decorating the day after Thanksgiving so we have a whole month to enjoy it."

"You haven't decorated in years," Otis spoke first. "Not since—ow." He glared at Wiley. "Why'd you kick me?"

Wiley didn't say anything, but even Becca could see the silent signal he was giving Otis to shut it. Of course, Gail hadn't decorated since her husband died, and probably even before that, when it became clear Amy wasn't coming home.

Gail smiled. "You're right, Otis, and there's no need for violence, Wiley, however well intended. But this year," she said, glancing at Noah, who was trying to peek under the table, probably hoping to get in on the kicking action, "I think a certain little munchkin might like to have the place look a bit festive."

Becca's heart sank. Not sure what to say, she put the dishes in the sink and got out the bowl of fresh whipped cream from the fridge. Surely Gail knew they weren't going to be here until Christmas.

Becca had to get back to work while she still had a job. She'd told Warren it would be at least a week, but maybe a few days more. He'd understood up to a point. She still didn't know what she would do if Amy didn't call soon. Other than have a heart-to-heart with the Mitchells. Her stomach churned at the thought.

Gail came up next to her with the pie in hand. "I know you won't be here all that long, but in the meantime, Noah and I will have a great time putting up the lights and decorations."

Becca smiled. "I'm sure he'll love it."

Ducking her head, she made sure Noah was still sitting on his booster seat. Ryder and Wiley were collecting the rest of the dishes.

As soon as Ryder entered the kitchen, Gail said, "I hope you have time to go get us a tree tomorrow." She raised her voice enough to carry into the dining room. "I bet I know a little boy who'd like to go with you."

Noah quit fidgeting and brought his head up. "What?"

"Uncle Ryder is going to go find us a Christmas tree tomorrow," Gail said, then darted her son a look. "Isn't he?"

Ryder smiled and nodded.

"He has to go into the forest, find the perfect one and cut it down." Gail frowned at the coffee maker. "Turn that on, would you, Becca?"

Becca closed the dishwasher and leaned over to flip the switch on the coffee maker. At the same time, she sneaked a peek at her phone on the counter, tucked out of the way. No missed calls.

"Uncle Ryder, you cut it down yourself?" Noah asked.

"That's right," he said, going back to the table for the

serving bowls. "It's tradition. Except this year, you're going to help me."

Noah couldn't contain himself. He climbed down from his booster chair and started jumping up and down all over the dining room. "I choose the tree. I choose the tree! I cut it down?"

"Maybe not by yourself," Ryder said. "You can choose the one you want, then watch me bring it down."

Noah didn't even pout. Just kept bouncing in his excitement.

Becca started to tell him to cool it, but Gail must've read her mind. She touched Becca's arm and whispered, "He's fine."

"Probably driving Otis nuts."

"Good," Wiley said and set the platter with the leftover turkey on the counter.

Gail and Becca looked at each other and laughed.

"If you're around tomorrow, Wiley, I could use your help stringing up lights," Gail said, stopping him halfway back to the dining room.

"Well, Ms. Gail, you know it would be my pleasure." He poked a finger in the air, where the brim of his hat would've been if he were wearing it.

Becca turned away, biting her lip, refusing to look at Ryder. Instead, she focused on Noah.

It hadn't snowed yet, but it might before they went back to LA, and he'd never actually seen it snow, so that would be another treat…

Her thoughts came to a sudden halt.

She had to stop assuming Noah would be leaving with her. Each new day confirmed what she'd already known deep in her heart.

The Mitchells were a fine family and Noah belonged with them. He was like a different boy out here. She hadn't realized how much he loved being around animals. And riding on an ATV was, according to him, like flying, and he couldn't get enough of it. Running with the cows in the pasture, running everywhere with nobody to clip his wings had been better than any gift she could ever give him.

How could she even think about taking him away from all this? Her eyes started to mist and she blinked hard, refusing to ruin the holiday.

With the table almost cleared, she took out the dessert plates and the pie server and put them all down on the counter while Gail retrieved the box from the bakery.

Otis put up a hand when Becca set a plate in front of him. "None for me, thanks."

"You love my pumpkin pie," Gail said.

"I'll get my slice tomorrow, if it's all the same to you."

Ryder met his mom's gaze. "He's got his own tradition to tend to."

"Of course. Silly me." Gail shook her head. "Your moonshine."

Ryder laughed as he looked at Becca's face. "Just wait till you taste Otis's brew. It's legendary around these parts."

"Um, I can't even handle beer, remember?"

Gail glanced from Becca to Ryder. "Did I miss something?"

"What's moooshine?" Noah asked. "Something for the cows?"

Becca was glad to let her blush settle while she put him back in his booster seat. "It's a grown-up's drink. Are you ready for dessert?"

He screwed up his expression as if she'd asked him a trick question. "Is it pie?" he whispered.

Gail walked over to them, and with great showmanship, opened the white box to reveal an oversize cupcake with a frosted turkey on top. Chocolate, of course. Noah's favorite.

"That's all for me?"

"You'll have some tonight and some tomorrow," Becca said, not wanting to deal with a sick little boy all night. "What do you say?"

He looked up at Gail with twinkling eyes, as if she'd given him the moon itself. "Thank you, Aunt Gail. It's my favorite ever."

Becca's heart ripped again. She was caught between the biggest rock and the hardest place on earth, and she wasn't sure how she was going to fix it. She didn't want anyone to suffer because of her, but maybe it was her destiny to carry one more burden. One that would haunt her the rest of her life.

"You coming with us to pick out the tree?" Ryder asked, so close he was able to whisper, his breath warm on her neck.

A little shiver ran down her spine. "No. That seems like a good time to go to my grandparents' house. See what kind of shape it's in. It might be a little emotional for me, and I'd rather do it on my own."

Ryder gave his mom an odd look, and then he nodded.

"I don't think there's electricity in the house," Gail said. "The water is probably still hooked up, but it's been over a year since your mother's been by."

"Ah, thanks, I wasn't sure. It's good that I'll be going while it's light out. I know she put aside some things for me, like the quilt Grams made for me, and there were some pictures I wanted." Becca shrugged. "I'm not expecting much. Mom told me she'd donated most of the furniture to the senior center."

"I think it sounds like the perfect time to go," Ryder said. "You won't have to worry about Noah."

Wiley opened his mouth to say something, but Gail clearly had something else in mind. She took him by the hand and led him to his seat. "I think you should dole out the whipped cream, and no taking the lion's share this year, my friend."

Becca wondered if anyone else had noticed. That was, anyone besides Ryder. Gail hadn't used her cane once the whole evening.

AFTER THE DISHWASHER was loaded, the food was all put away and his mom had gone to her room, Ryder decided to have a shot of his dad's favorite brandy. But he wanted Becca to join him. Although she'd probably be completely wasted after one sip.

He grinned, thinking about her schoolgirl crush. He hadn't given her much thought back then, so it was odd how he'd remembered so much. He'd been more concerned with college and Leanne, and knowing that he'd be running the ranch someday. He sure wished his dad were here to see how much the place had grown, and how well they were doing. But Ryder supposed his dad knew it anyway.

When he got to the living room, he poured two small glasses of brandy as he waited for Becca, who was taking a while putting Noah to bed. But then Noah had been filled with sugar and excitement over tomorrow's adventure and was probably fighting sleep.

Ryder figured having one more brandy wouldn't hurt, then relaxed on the couch, skipping his usual spot in the recliner.

Tonight's celebration had been almost like old times. He wished his whole family could have been there, but he was glad they'd had Becca and Noah. That kid was a little firecracker. He didn't just light up a room, he'd brought life back to the Sundowner.

Despite all the jumping and the many questions, he was a bright boy with a real spirit of adventure. Ryder had thought a city kid would be hesitant and awkward with the unfamiliar countryside and animals only seen on TV, but not Noah.

Partly, Ryder suspected, because of Becca. She was really something—young in some ways, yet wise beyond her years, reliable, considerate, strong. She sure hadn't taken any of his crap. The more he got to know the adult version of Becca, the more interested he was in exploring something beyond friendship.

When she finally joined him, he could see worry in her expression, hesitation in her step.

He stood. "Is Noah all right?"

"What? Yes, he's finally calmed down enough to sleep. He's so excited about tomorrow, and tonight was very special."

"You're worried about something."

She sighed, looked into his eyes, then away. "I thought Amy would have called by now. You know how much she loves holidays. She used to always keep in touch, and well, it bothers me."

Ryder thought about giving Becca the brandy, but instead put his arm around her shoulder. "It's been a while since she's cared about the holidays. At least from my perspective. You know she's called here before when she was drunk. Or high. Not all the time, but enough for us to realize she wasn't exactly herself."

Becca's wince didn't surprise him, but it made things a little more clear. She had responsibilities she couldn't ignore. Amy's life had obviously turned down a different road. He was glad, though, that the two women were still friends. Probably due to Becca's loyalty, as he was beginning to see.

"Maybe she just got a little too festive tonight," he suggested, "and she'll call tomorrow."

Becca didn't seem convinced. If anything, she looked even more concerned.

"You don't think so?"

"I don't know," she said. "I'm worried about her."

"So am I. But there's not much we can do tonight."

"No," Becca said, clearly trying to appear more at ease. "Not tonight."

"So how about you try a little drink? Just a small one. My father's favorite brandy."

Her expression, one that told him he wasn't going to take her on that ride again, made him laugh. And then she smiled.

Time seemed to stop as their gazes held. He'd tightened his arm around her without even realizing it. All he had to do was lower his head a few inches for their mouths to meet. The very tip of Becca's pink tongue slipped out to moisten her lips.

Damn, he wanted to kiss her.

"By the way," he said. "I know you lied."

She blinked, before her eyes widened. She backed away and he had no choice but to lower his arm. "What do you mean?"

Goddamn it.

Yeah, he was real slick. Great way to set the mood.

"That came out wrong. I know you were covering for her. You told my mom Amy was still bartending. I knew she'd quit. She told me herself a year ago. I didn't think my mom needed to know, so I'm glad you covered."

The explanation hadn't put Becca at ease like he'd

hoped. Her gaze kept darting toward the short hall to Gail's room.

"Mom went to bed a while ago. She didn't hear that. I promise."

Becca just nodded. "You know what? I'm pretty wiped out." She offered him a forced smile. "I think I'll turn in, too."

She didn't give him a second to respond. Before he could open his mouth, she was racing up the stairs.

Chapter Thirteen

Becca climbed out of her car, the engine still rattling, and looked at her old home. It wasn't very big, just a modest three-bedroom, one-bath, with a nice-sized kitchen and a living room that had been the center of her family life for nine years.

That single bathroom had been at the hub of a lot of ruffled feathers—mostly hers—when she'd hit her teens. But her memories were almost all good ones. Even through her parents' divorce, she'd found great solace and joy in her grandparents. They'd been her staunchest advocates, her biggest fans.

Of course her mother loved her, but at heart, Katie was a woman in search of something larger than herself. She'd wanted to matter.

That probably accounted for her marriage to Becca's father. A military life had taken Katie out into the big world and given her a credo she could stand behind. But she hadn't counted on the loneliness.

Becca looked out at the old barn where they used to keep their milk cow and the chickens. It hadn't been that color red when she'd last seen it. Or maybe she wasn't remembering correctly. As she walked closer to the barn, she saw the paint didn't look too old. But then, it had only been a couple of years since…

She pulled back her thoughts. She hadn't even stepped inside the house; she wasn't about to start crying already. There were too many good things to remember today. Noah was out having the time of his life choosing a Christmas tree. Gail was going through the ornaments and decorations, promising hot cocoa when they all returned.

Otis was out for the day, too, pouring his moonshine. The still hadn't blown up, which Becca hadn't realized could happen. But according to Ryder, it not only could but had once, many years ago, when Otis was still a young man. If Amy had told her about it, she didn't remember.

The thought of Amy lowered her spirits, but Becca closed her eyes and focused on something else. Last night. She and Ryder in the living room, his arm around her, and a moment that had warmed her all the way to her toes. Until he'd nearly given her a heart attack.

Good thing she hadn't asked which lie he meant.

Later though, after Becca had changed into her nightshirt and slipped into bed, she'd rekindled the wonderful, safe feeling of having his arm around her. She was pretty darn sure he'd been thinking about kissing her. She was equally sure she would've kissed him back.

And after that? She hadn't dared fill in the blanks.

Remembering the heat of his chest and the strength of his arm made her warm even now as she opened the door to a past that felt both ancient and like it had happened yesterday.

If only Grams were still here, Becca would have confessed everything to her. All of it. The promises she'd broken, the love she'd found in Noah, the heartache of Amy's decline and her own helplessness.

She'd have confessed her feelings for Ryder. How

they'd grown by the day, and the impossibility of her situation. Knowing that there was unimaginable pain in her future, no matter how the lies played out.

Grams would have comforted her and loved her all the same.

Becca breathed out as she crossed the threshold of her grandparents' house. Home, but not.

It was almost empty. The living room had no couch, just Grandpa's recliner. That had been ready for the landfill for ages, but he'd been too attached to the old thing. It no longer reclined, and one side of the seat was bent out of shape.

She could still see him in it. His white rim of hair, his kind smile. It was chilly without electricity, but the windows, despite the dust, let in enough light to see all she needed to. The old wood-burning stove looked to be in good shape. And there was still a half cord of logs in the old copper bathtub that had been there since before she and her mom had arrived in Blackfoot Falls.

But the pictures on the mantel were gone. Becca could only hope that her mother had boxed them up with the quilt and the pillows Grams had made to go with Becca's old room. The collectable bells Grams had loved were also absent. Nothing special, just souvenirs from her travels, which had held a place of pride on a shelf above the mantel.

The grandfather clock wasn't against the far wall, and that made Becca sad. It wasn't valuable or anything, but it had belonged to her great grandfather and she'd loved the sound of the bongs throughout the house.

Of course, she wouldn't have room for it in her place in LA. She would barely have room for the quilt.

In her old bedroom, the bed and dresser were gone. So was the old rug she'd made in school. But inside the closet, the boxes her mother had packed for her were labeled with Becca's name and stacked high, the old rug right on top.

Wouldn't it be something if she could move back here? She'd put the bells back on a new shelf, and find a couch that was as comfortable as the old green one she'd loved.

She'd make this room up for Noah. He'd like the window seat, where he could look out at the trees and watch the seasons change. No canopy bed for him, though. He'd want something with cars or trucks.

Then again, maybe he'd want something with horses.

She'd never find a job that would pay enough to support the two of them and pay for the upkeep of the house, let alone the land. She wasn't sure how her mother was managing, given she mostly volunteered, but maybe Becca's grandparents had left her something so she could keep the ranch in the family.

Living there would be a lot cheaper than Los Angeles. Living on Mars would be less expensive. Oh, how Noah would love growing up here. So close to the Mitchells' ranch.

Maybe she would find a way to get him his own horse someday. And maybe she wouldn't feel so guilty all the time. Living here could be a happy medium…giving him the family he didn't know was his own, but letting her still be his mother.

Becca sighed.

Maybe she should start living in reality.

She had no right leaving Gail and Ryder in the dark. Even if Amy suddenly called, she couldn't offer Noah a safe environment. The Mitchells would and should step in on Noah's behalf.

By keeping the secret, Becca wasn't just screwing them over, she was hurting herself. Her mindset needed to reboot. Every time she had a thought about her and Noah returning to LA together, she was lying to herself.

And Ryder?

Just thinking about him made her heart skip a beat. The relationship that was slowly forming between them was something she'd never expected.

Of course, nothing could ever really happen between them. Not while she was being so deceitful. Telling the truth wouldn't be any better. They'd probably forbid her from seeing Noah again. And they wouldn't be wrong.

She sat down on the wood floor and pulled out a box, taking every item out for inspection, one by one. It was comforting and sad, which was better than thinking about her uncertain future.

By the time she'd repacked everything, she'd used up several tissues and decided the best thing to do while she had privacy was to make some phone calls. First, Isabella.

She answered quickly. "Becca. I've been waiting to hear from you. I've been worried."

"Didn't you get my text?"

"Four days ago."

"Really?" *Four days?* Becca rubbed her forehead. "I'm so sorry. I can't seem to keep track of time. You know, you can call me. Anytime. If I can't talk, I'll call back."

"Okay, I'm glad to know that. Fortunately I don't have anything to report. I've been keeping an eye on the house. No sign that Derek's been around. Has he called you again?"

"Once. He sounded high. Like, really messed up."

"That's good."

In spite of everything, Becca laughed. "I thought the same thing. He went to the restaurant a day after we left, but not since then. I know the manager pretty well. She promised to call if he shows up again."

"Good. Have you heard from Amy?" Something in Isabella's voice put Becca on edge.

"No. Has she been by the house?"

"Not that I know of. I even asked the neighborhood punks… You know, the ones that hang out at the corner. They haven't seen her."

"Oh, good Lord, please don't get mixed up with them. I'm already so scared for Amy. I don't want to add you to the list." She'd already involved Isabella too much in her life. Now that Derek was a threat, Becca had to be especially careful not to lean on her friend, even though Isabella had always been there for her.

"Don't worry about me," Isabella said with a short laugh. "I gave them a twenty for the information. It was business. That, they understand." Isabella paused. "Have you made any decisions?"

Becca sank against the wall. "I don't know what to do. I'd be back tomorrow if I didn't have Noah to think about."

"It's probably best you stay there for a little while longer. Maybe Amy is just fine, but to be honest, my gut tells me otherwise."

"Mine does, too. Oh, Isabella." The tears were falling again, and she didn't have any tissues left. "Maybe I shouldn't have come. Maybe I should have told Noah's family everything and gone right back to LA without him."

"He's your son, *querida mia*. You've been a good mother to him from the first day he was born. You've done everything you could to help Amy. But she let the drugs and that bastard steal her soul. I can't think of any friend who could have done more."

"I hope that's true."

"How is Noah enjoying the wild West?"

"He's loving every minute of it. I should have taken a million pictures by now, and I haven't. I'll have to make up for it in the time I've got left."

"Enjoy him for all it's worth. Stay for a while. I'll do what I can to find out about Amy and Derek. I want you two to be safe."

"You need to stay safe, too. What would we do without you?"

"I'll be fine. Now go back to your boy and take pictures!"

"I promise. I'll call you when I know more."

They disconnected, but Becca just sat there on the floor, letting a few more tears fall. As she got up to get another pack of tissues from the car, she received a text. It was from her boss, who she'd planned on calling.

Of course, he wanted to know what her plans were. And when she'd be back to work.

Instead of taking the easy way out with a text, she returned his call.

Warren answered with, "I hope it's good news."

"I wish it could be better, but it looks like I'll be here another week."

His silence didn't bode well. "That's unfortunate, Becca. We have deadlines to meet. And you still have a lot to learn."

"I know, Warren. And I do want to learn it all. I love the new position, but this really is a family emergency, and I'm doing my best to take care of everything so I can come back as quickly as possible."

"I'm counting on it. Do you at least have an idea when you'll be back?"

Becca held in a sigh. "I'll let you know the minute I'm sure."

"Fair enough. And I am sorry for your situation."

She disconnected, knowing it could have gone a lot worse. Apparently her stomach hadn't gotten the message. It was a roiling mess. She was lucky to have that job. Without a college education, her options were limited. To have gone from waitress to management was more than she'd ever expected.

But it was time to go back to the ranch. For all she knew, Noah and the tree were already there.

She ended up following Ryder's truck, with an enormous Douglas fir tied down in the back. She knew Noah was buckled into his car seat, but she also knew he'd be hopping like a jackrabbit the moment he was free. She parked behind them and pulled out her cell phone, ready to capture everything so she'd remember this day. This visit. This world.

In no time, Ryder had Noah out and jumping around as if he'd dealt with a car seat all his life.

Noah ran up and crashed into her so hard she stumbled. "Lookit, Mommy! My tree!"

"That's a monster. How are you going to carry it into the house?"

"I'm real strong. I carried some rope the whole time." He saw Ryder and Lance untying the tree and made a dash for the truck, but she stopped him before he could get underfoot. "Let's wait right here until the tree is in the house. I'd hate to have you squashed before you help Aunt Gail decorate."

He didn't run, but he did jump.

Ryder grinned as he and Lance wrestled the fir off the bed to the ground. It was so huge, she had to wonder if it would even fit through the doorway.

"Let's go inside and warm up while I figure out if I have to cut any more off this brute," Ryder said. "Besides, I know there's hot cocoa ready."

"Me, too!" Noah yelled as if Ryder were miles away. "I'll be first." Now, he did run, almost knocking Wiley over.

"Noah, walk!"

He was inside before her warning got to him, and she scurried to catch up, but Ryder slowed her down with a hand on her arm. "He's fine," he said. "In fact, he was good the entire time. He's running on adrenaline now. But trust me, I wore him out."

"It looks like he returned the favor."

"I won't deny it. He sure does know how to pick good trees, though."

"I'll bet he asked a thousand questions before he made his final choice."

Ryder winked. "A thousand and one."

"Thanks for being so patient with him. Not that I'm surprised. You were always patient with me."

His grimace made it look as if he'd been kicked in the gut. "It's not easy thinking of you as that kid anymore," he said, the heat in his eyes making it very clear what he thought of her now.

"Oh. That's good. I guess."

He smiled, then glanced back. Everyone had disappeared. "Look, Becca, I'm sorry. I was wrong about you. I should've apologized sooner. But Amy—well, she's my—"

"Please." Becca saw he was struggling. This time, she touched his arm. "You don't need to explain. Truly. I've blamed myself, too, wondering if I could've done more."

"You're an amazing woman, you know that?"

Becca blushed and would've pulled her hand back if he'd let her. "No. I'm not. Trust me."

"That's the thing, I do trust you. I don't have a single doubt you've been loyal to my sister. She's lucky to have you." His fingers trailed down her arm, then he squeezed her hand. It was more of a caress than simple reassurance. "I'm lucky, too," he said. "That you're here and giving me another chance."

Becca's chest hurt and she was afraid she couldn't get enough air.

"Yes, I know I'm not your first priority," he said with a crooked smile. "You're here because of Noah and my mom."

"That's not the only reason." She heard herself speak but couldn't believe she'd dared to say anything. She wasn't at all trustworthy, as he'd soon discover. But they'd turned a corner, it seemed. Maybe he would understand. "I'm glad we can be friends again."

"Friends." Ryder slowly nodded as he held her gaze. "It's a start."

"Mommy!" Noah was out of sight, but everyone within a mile had probably heard him. "Hurry!"

Becca broke eye contact first. She didn't know if she should laugh or cry.

THE MOMENT THEY walked into the house, the smell of pine was replaced by his mother's from-scratch cocoa. It had always been a favorite, and it brought back memories of his childhood. Of Becca when she used to hang out in the stable.

"Are you a marshmallow man, or do you take your cocoa neat?" she asked.

He was relieved he hadn't made things awkward between them. And not a bit sorry he'd given her something to think about. "Two, and none of those minis. I want the real—"

"Mommy, Aunt Gail says I have to ask you if I can have two marshmallows like Uncle Ryder gets."

"First of all, young man, remember you're not supposed to interrupt adults. Uncle Ryder was speaking. What do you say?"

"Sorry, Uncle Ryder." The words were said so quickly they blurred together. Then he paused, wrinkling his nose. "Can I intrumpt kids?"

It was clear Becca was fighting a grin. "It's not polite to interrupt anyone, unless there's an emergency. Was your interruption an emergency?"

Noah's eyes widened. "Yes! The cocoa is ready. And the marshmallows are big!"

"You may have one, not two."

"Why not?"

"Because you're only four and one is plenty. When you're older, you can have two."

"How old?"

"Eighteen."

His expression fell and he looked as if she'd taken away his truck. "That's forever."

"Go get your cocoa before it gets cold," she said.

He huffed, just once, then dashed back to the kitchen.

"Eighteen?" Ryder asked.

"I'm quite sure this negotiation will come up before then. And once again, thank you. His questions can be exhausting."

"I honestly don't mind. I like having him around, and a curious kid is a healthy kid."

"That's true, but I think the whole lot of you will give a big sigh of relief when we're out of your hair."

Ryder wasn't so sure about that, and by the way she was studying him, he had to wonder if she was putting out feelers. Trying to figure out if he meant what he'd said outside. Or if she'd understood him correctly. Maybe he should've flat out told her how much he'd been thinking about how she'd felt in his arms, and how hard it had been not to kiss her last night.

"Hey, if it were up to me, you and Noah would move back home," he said, watching her fight a smile.

His heart thumped like he was a damn teenager.

"Mommy!"

They exchanged looks and grinned.

In the kitchen, Noah was already in his booster seat staring at the bobbing white glob in his cocoa. Lance had obviously slipped in through the back door and had a mug in hand.

Gail was getting ready to ladle out more from her big pot and smiled at Becca. "How do you take your cocoa?"

"Usually plain, but today feels like a one-marshmallow day."

"One it is." As Gail filled the mug, she said, "I need someone to go get the big bucket for the tree. From what Wiley said, we'll have to cut a hole in the roof to get it inside."

"I'll go," Becca offered.

Ryder shook his head. "You don't even know where it is. I'll go with."

"But the cocoa."

"It'll still be here when we get back," he said, steering her out the kitchen door.

Inside the barn, Becca stopped short at the variety of buckets stacked under the stairs to the loft. She pulled one out. Then another larger one. Then a slightly smaller one. Her nose wrinkled like Noah's as she tried to pick the right size.

"You're overthinking this. But hell, it's clear you're good at your R & D job. A real detail woman. Not satisfied with just any solution. It has to be the right one."

She looked blankly at him. "I'm going to take that as a compliment."

"Good. That's how I meant it."

He'd moved closer to her, close enough to take the two buckets out of her hands, and it occurred to him that she might've been stalling. One way to find out.

He leaned in and kissed her. His lips on hers, nothing overly dramatic, just a test run. When he dropped the buckets and broke it off, she looked disappointed.

Ryder pulled her into his arms and kissed her like he'd wanted to last night and all this morning. Hell, like he'd wanted to when they'd come back from town.

She fit like she'd been designed to rest against his chest. Even with their damn coats. Which he wanted to unzip right now and throw on the haystack. But that might have to wait because the way she tasted, a little like peppermint and a lot like want, was absorbing all of his attention.

A second later, she jerked back a bit, grabbed a breath, then tilted her head. But this time it wasn't exactly smooth sailing. Her nose bumped his, and it threw her off. She leaned back and looked at him as if she wasn't sure what to do.

He offered a little help and once he cupped her nape with his palm, they found their rhythm again. But he could feel how rapidly her heart was beating. He hoped he hadn't overstepped. He wanted this to be the first of many, but he backed off just in case.

"You okay?"

She nodded quickly, a smile teasing her lips.

"You don't want to slap my face or anything?"

She laughed, then leaned in and grabbed one more brief kiss. Her shy smile and that trademark blush told him everything was fine. Oddly, though, he was reminded of his early high school days with Maggie Weaver. With both of them new at making out, they'd fumbled around like eager puppies. Which was kind of crazy. Becca was twenty-five, and she had a child. Still, he had the feeling she wasn't very experienced.

For some stupid reason, the idea pleased him. He squeezed her hand, then picked up the biggest bucket. "We better get back in there before I get carried away."

Even in the barn's dim light, Becca's eyes shined. Yeah, there'd be more kissing. He touched her hair, stroked her cheek with his thumb.

"How long have we been out here?" she whispered, her lids drifting closed.

"Not long," he said, amazed at the softness of her skin. He slipped his fingers into her hair and her breathy sigh skimmed his wrist. At the renewed urge to strip off both their jackets, he snapped out of it. "Maybe too long. Come on."

With his hand on the small of her back, he guided her out of the barn, grateful for the chilly air. His body needed to settle down before they reached the house.

Thankfully, everyone was still in the kitchen. Becca stepped to the side as he studied the ceiling, trying to guesstimate if the huge fir would fit. Somehow, he'd make it happen. But not if his thoughts kept straying back to Becca and the kiss. When he glanced at her, he saw that she'd been staring at him. They smiled at each other.

Then Lance walked out of the kitchen. "What can I do, boss?"

Ryder finally got the bucket where it needed to be—not too close to the fireplace. "Help me move these two chairs," he said, "so we can bring in the tree. Where's Wiley?"

"Getting something from the bunkhouse. He'll be right back."

The setup was perfect. With help, he'd get that sucker inside. He turned for the door, just as someone knocked. He saw the tan uniform through the decorative glass and thought it might be Grace, but what would the sheriff be doing at their place?

"Afternoon, Sheriff," he said, as he opened the door. Ryder could see from her expression it wasn't a holiday call. There was no doubt at all that it was bad news. Real bad news.

Chapter Fourteen

Becca started shaking the moment she saw the woman in uniform enter the living room. *Nonononono* screamed in her head.

Gail came from the kitchen through the dining room, distracting Becca for a moment. Then Wiley burst through the front door, his breath coming out in heaves as he went to stand by Gail.

Ryder, who looked tense but together, moved closer to Noah who was staring at the sheriff with his mouth open. She gave him a brief smile, a small nod at Becca, then addressed Ryder in a quiet voice. "We should speak in private."

He frowned absently, evidently lost in his own thoughts. "Sheriff, this is Becca Hartman, she's a family friend. It's okay for her to be here."

"Hi, I'm Grace," the sheriff said, then glanced at Noah. "What about the boy?"

"Becca, please stay," Gail said, a beat behind, her voice shaky. She looked at Wiley.

He looked torn, but then scooped up Noah. "Lance and me need some help figuring out where to put the outdoor lights, little man, and since you did such a great job choosing the tree…"

Wiley already had him at the door, with Lance on his heels. A second later, the door closed behind them.

"Why don't we all take a seat?" Grace said.

Ryder went to Gail's side, and when her knees started to buckle, he helped her walk to the couch where he sat her down next to him, leaving space for Becca on his other side. His arm went around his mother.

Grace took a seat on the edge of the chair across from the couch, her hat in her hands, her expression so full of sorrow there was no doubt what had happened—just the how.

"I'm so sorry to have to tell you this," she began. "The LAPD believe they've found your daughter. Amy had her driver's license on her and the picture was a match."

Gail's cry filled the living room. It wrenched Becca's heart, and she didn't hear her own cry until the sob that followed.

"How?" Ryder asked, his voice so low and cold it was like the north wind slicing into Becca's skin.

"Beaten and strangled, as far as they know. The medical examiner hasn't issued a statement yet."

"Where did they find her?"

"In a park close to the address listed on her license."

Ryder stared down for a moment. "I guess there's no chance they made a mistake." He looked up. "How did they know to contact you?"

"She was in the system," Grace said and cleared her throat. "She also had a couple of pictures on her. One of a little boy. And a high school yearbook photo of her and two friends that pointed them to Blackfoot Falls."

Becca gasped.

It was Noah in that picture. Her Noah. Amy's Noah.

She doubled over on the couch, wracked with pain so deep the sound was trapped inside her chest, squeezing the life right out of her. The bastard had killed her. Becca knew he had. Yet she felt so utterly unprepared. As if she hadn't suspected a thing. Hadn't imagined this moment a hundred times.

All she could see behind her closed eyes was Amy that last day, the determination to escape on her face. The way she'd looked at Noah.

The front door opened. It was Wiley. "Otis has Noah," he said. "He's fine." He went over to the couch and rested on the arm next to Gail. She lifted a trembling hand, and he grabbed it.

Ryder nodded at the older man. "It's about Amy."

Wiley didn't look away from Gail, not even for a second. Her head was down as she quietly sobbed into her other hand.

Becca, her vision blurred with tears, could barely believe how Ryder was so in control. How he wasn't ripping the room to shreds.

Briefly, he bowed his head. "Do they have any suspects?"

"They didn't say. Her body is with the Los Angeles County coroner's office, where they'll perform an autopsy. But they'll need one of you to go and give an official identification before they can proceed." Grace caught Ryder's eye and some sort of silent communication passed between them.

"Thank you," he said. "Anything else?"

Grace stood, taking a piece of paper out of her breast pocket and passing it to Ryder. "That's the phone number and address of the coroner's office. I've included the name and number of the investigating officer and my card with my cell phone number if you need anything."

Ryder rose, leaving Wiley to tend to his mother while

he walked the sheriff to the door. "Thanks for coming, Grace. I know this wasn't easy for you either."

"I'm just so sorry for all of you. I didn't know Amy, but I've heard she was a nice person." She hesitated at the door and glanced at Becca, who'd followed them. "Is there anyone else I can call?"

"No," he said, sounding bone-weary. "I'll take care of everything from here."

"Look, Ryder, I don't know you that well, but personally, let me just say, your mom shouldn't go to LA."

"I know."

Grace shook his hand, nodded at Becca and left.

"Wait." Becca caught Ryder's arm when he turned toward his mom. "I need to talk to you."

He gestured to give him a moment.

They watched as Wiley helped Gail to her feet, put his arm around her shoulder. "Come on, Gail. Let's go get you a glass of water."

Ryder might've said something, done something to signal Wiley, but Gail didn't put up much of a fight. Becca didn't think she had anything left to fight with. But before Gail entered the kitchen, she turned to Ryder. "I'll go," she said, her voice older than her years. "I'll go get ready."

It was quiet when Wiley helped her into the kitchen, releasing the swinging door behind him.

As soon as they were alone, Becca said, "The sheriff is right. Your mom can't go. And neither should you. I'll go to LA and make the ID." She moved her hand to her stomach, afraid she was going to be sick. "Amy won't look how you remember her. She hasn't been in good shape for a while." She touched his arm. "Please. I don't want that to be your last memory of her."

He looked into her eyes and she could see he wasn't

calm at all. His eyes were so full of shocked rage. "You left her. You knew she was in trouble, and you left her to face it alone. You should've told us the truth so I could have done something. I could have gone to get her. Brought her back. Put her into rehab. She'd still be alive."

Becca flinched. Some part of her brain knew she couldn't have told them anything. She didn't know where Amy was living or how she'd planned to get away from Derek. Becca had tried to help her, but their only communication had been on Amy's terms. What was Becca supposed to have done? She hadn't called the family because she'd believed Amy's lies. And most important of all, Becca's first concern had to be Noah.

But she couldn't say any of that to Ryder. "I'll go to Los Angeles. I'll identify her. And I'll talk to the investigating officer."

"Oh," he said, his voice like fire and ice, "you're going all right. And so am I."

He turned his back on her and pushed open the kitchen door so hard she was surprised it didn't break off the hinges.

Becca ran to the bathroom, sure now that she was going to be sick. It seemed everything she'd feared had come true. Except it hadn't occurred to her that Ryder could hate her so very much. That Gail would never want to look at her again. It was her fault. All of it. She should have tried harder, done more to get Amy free from the drugs and Derek.

She landed on her knees, in front of the toilet, and even though she'd had a small breakfast, it burned coming up. Or maybe that was just what it felt like now to be her. Burning pain, scorching guilt.

Finally, when there was nothing left in her, she washed her face, cleaned her mouth. She had to go out there. The only thought that made it possible to move was that Noah was safe. Her sacrifice was worth that, at least. Even if it wasn't close to being enough.

Stepping into the hallway, she passed the pictures of young Amy in the frames on the wall. Her tears started again, and she supposed they'd never stop. The living room was empty. The bucket for the Christmas tree was still by the front window.

The kitchen door opened and Ryder emerged, shutting the door behind him.

She walked over to him, stood as straight as possible in front of his condemning gaze. "I need to go back, anyway. Noah will come with me. I have someone to look after him while I take care of everything, so you can be here for your mother. You're both wounded and grieving."

Ryder snorted. "You think I'd trust you to go alone? And besides, you don't have time for your *best friend's* funeral? You're going to cut and run now? Bullshit. You're coming with me. We'll leave Noah right here."

It was a slap so hard it knocked her back to six days ago. Her panic was just as real as it had been when she'd done everything in her power to get Noah out of LA and beyond Derek's reach. "I'm not leaving him."

"Yes, you are."

"No." She turned around, ready to race to the bunkhouse. All she needed was him and her purse. The hell with their things.

Ryder caught her arm. "You planning on running? Huh? You'd rip him away from my mother *now*? When she needs the comfort?"

His words got to her. "Noah and I have never been apart," she whispered, twisting her arm to get free. "What am I going to say to him?"

He looked down, somewhat startled, and quickly released her. "Don't worry about it. My mother will explain."

"No. It's my responsibility."

"You have some nerve talking about responsibility now."

"Ryder. I'm his—"

"Mother? Like you were Amy's friend? We have to be at the Kalispell airport before dawn. I've already gotten the tickets."

THE DRIVE TO the coroner's office had been worse than he'd imagined. He'd been to LA before, but he'd never flown into LAX or driven in rush hour traffic. It didn't help that, now, two hours since making the identification, they were still driving at a snail's pace and hadn't spoken. He would've welcomed the silence but it made it too easy to recall Amy's lifeless, bruised and battered face.

Jesus, he'd give just about anything to get a hold of the bastard who'd killed her before the cops got to him.

Becca shifted in the passenger seat. According to the coroner's office, the police wanted to ask her some questions about Amy's boyfriend, and she seemed eager to speak with them. Or maybe that's what she wanted Ryder to believe.

She'd tried to convince him to go check into a hotel while she took a cab to the LAPD office. As if he would let her out of his sight. Who the hell knew what she was going to tell the detective? Something twitched inside his gut at that thought, but just because he'd been attracted to her, and Noah was a great kid, didn't mean Becca was a good person.

Good people didn't go on the run while their friends were in the crosshairs of some drug dealer.

The Hollenbeck PD in Boyle Heights had a fancy façade, but it was surrounded by a lot of brick buildings and graffiti. Ryder sat with Becca in the lobby, waiting for far too long in the uncomfortable silence to be called into an empty office by the investigating officer.

He was a tall, slender Latino man by the name of Alfonso Richardson, who offered them a beverage, then sat down across from them.

He flipped open a file and read for a minute, then looked at Becca. "You're related to Amy Mitchell?"

"I am," Ryder said.

"But I live here and was Amy's friend."

"In Los Angeles?"

Becca nodded. "Boyle Heights, actually. Soto Street."

"Do you know who would have wanted to hurt Ms. Mitchell?"

Becca sniffed, fisting the tissue in her hand. "I know her boyfriend was Derek Gomes. I know he's a drug dealer, and he was responsible for Amy getting into drugs."

"You'd met him? Been to their apartment?"

"I met him about six years ago. Saw him a few times after that. But Amy—" Becca glanced down. "Amy knew I didn't like him, so after she moved in with him, she always came to my house or we met somewhere. I don't know where their apartment is. She didn't want me getting mixed up with his friends. I did see Derek a couple of times, though. Near Sam's Tacos."

"Were you aware that Ms. Mitchell showed signs of abuse going back months, maybe years?"

"Yes," she said, then paused before she could speak again. "I didn't see the bruises at first, she hid them well, but I knew they were there." Tears slid down her cheeks, but she wiped them away with the back of her hand and used the crumpled tissue for her nose. "I did everything

I could to get her to leave him… I did. But she wouldn't go. She said she would, but she never tried. Until a few days before I left town."

"What happened?"

Ryder sat forward in his chair.

"She came over. Brought my—" Her voice broke. She bowed her head, dabbing furiously at her eyes. Started to speak, then stopped again. It sounded as though she couldn't catch her breath.

Even Ryder got a little worried for her.

"Are you okay?" the detective asked. "Would you like to take a break?"

Keeping her gaze lowered, she shook her head.

He glanced at Ryder. "Ms. Hartman, would you prefer we conduct this interview in private?"

Like hell.

Ryder was about to set the cop straight when Becca shook her head, her hair falling forward and hiding most of her face.

"Amy brought my son a toy and gave me some money. Not a lot, a few hundred dollars, but I didn't want to take it when she told me she was leaving Derek. She said he was in trouble with some guys, I guess his drug suppliers. And that he had to go to the border to take care of business. He'd never let her out of his sight for more than a couple of hours before. But he wasn't taking her with him, and she figured it would be the only chance she'd have to get as far away as she could."

The detective kept writing as she took a sip of water.

"I tried to get her to go to a women's shelter. I mapped them out for her and explained that Derek wouldn't be able to get to her in any of them, but she just wouldn't."

"How did the two of you leave things?"

"She was supposed to get a burner phone after she'd

left him and call me. But it wasn't her that called. It was Derek. And he was…furious. I think he thought she was staying with me, but he didn't know where I lived." Her eyes were painfully bloodshot when she looked at Ryder.

"Anything else?" the man asked in a gentle tone that drew her attention back to him.

"She never said what kind of trouble Derek was in. The last couple of years, all we talked about was our past, and sometimes how we wished we'd never left Montana. And Noah. My son. That's all. She was embarrassed about what had happened to her and changed the subject whenever I brought it up. I honestly don't know anything more about her life or Derek's dealing. I'm sorry. I would like to help. If anything I've said or know about Derek will help get him arrested, I'm willing to testify in court."

Detective Richardson studied her a moment, then smiled. "You're a brave woman. Cartels are big on payback."

"I'm not brave. Amy deserves justice."

"He's right," Ryder said, urging her to look at him. "Testifying would be dangerous and you have Noah to think about."

"I would never put my son at risk." She held Ryder's gaze and for the first time since Grace had shown up at their door, Becca's eyes looked perfectly clear. "Noah has people who love him. If anything happened to me, he'd be able to grow up safe and happy, far away from all of this ugliness."

Ryder reached for her hand but reconsidered. "All I'm saying is that you really need to think hard about something like this."

"I have," she said with a wry laugh. "Believe me, I've thought about it a lot."

Just as Becca looked away, Detective Richardson said,

"Well, fortunately, you won't have to make that decision. When we went to the address on Ms. Mitchell's license, we found Gomes dead in his apartment. It was two days after it was estimated that Ms. Mitchell was killed. The autopsies will confirm those dates." He folded his hands on the file. "He was shot execution-style, with all the earmarks of a cartel hit. You've filled in a lot of missing pieces, Ms. Hartman, and I think we'll find that Ms. Mitchell did get her justice."

Becca's mouth quivered and tears rushed down her face. "But I failed her," she whispered. "She should still be alive."

"For what it's worth, I've been doing this job for too long, and it's made me more jaded than I care for. But you and your friend sound like remarkable women. I think she saved you from a lot of grief by not telling you what she knew. Despite the drug use, I'm thinking she was a good friend," Alfonso said, standing up. "And you never gave up on her. Four years is a long time to be a drug addict's friend, but you were there for her. Can't do more than that." He held out his hand. She shook it, and Ryder could see she was trembling badly.

"Thank you," she whispered, turned and stumbled to the door.

Ryder stayed close until they made it outside. Talk about an emotional roller coaster. He'd gotten angry all over again as he'd listened to her. Then she'd said something to make him swing the other way. The thing was, anger was a lot easier to hang onto.

While trying to remember where they'd parked the damn rental in a lot that would have held more cars than Blackfoot Falls had ever seen, he kept thinking about the time before Amy had met Gomes. Before she got in so deep. Becca had admitted they'd been disillusioned with LA. Even if Amy had been too stubborn to call, why hadn't Becca?

After they were on their way, Becca giving him directions in the hopelessly crowded city, he couldn't help remembering the detective's words. That Amy had saved Becca, and probably Noah, from harm. So at least he could tell his mother that Amy had been loyal to the end. That she might not have been able to save herself, but she'd tried her best to save Becca and Noah at the very least.

Jesus, the image of Amy's poor face. It kept creeping in when he didn't expect it. He figured he'd be haunted by that for the rest of his life. Both of them would, and he had to admit, he was a little ashamed that the detective had been more compassionate toward Becca than he had.

But her grief was no substitute for calling them before Amy had crossed the line. Becca knew them, they'd treated her like family. How hard would it have been for her to call?

Although, he'd heard the drugs in Amy's voice, the alcohol, the slurring. And he hadn't rushed to save her either. What kind of brother did that make him? What kind of man? Becca had been there when he hadn't. He'd failed Amy. And he didn't know how he was going to live with that.

He wasn't looking forward to the night ahead. Becca had warned him that her house was small. That it wasn't what he was used to. She'd been so nervous about him seeing it that he couldn't let it go. He had to know. See for himself. Just like he'd had to see his sister.

Tomorrow, they'd go back to the coroner's office, and he'd make the final arrangements for Amy's remains. He wasn't sure yet what he would do. God forbid his mother see her in that shape.

He'd have to think of something to tell her before they arrived at Becca's and he called home. But at the moment, what he really wanted was something to hit. Somewhere to shout until he lost his voice. Anything not to feel this helpless. And like a complete failure.

Chapter Fifteen

The street itself was in disrepair with more potholes than road, but when Ryder saw Becca's house, he finally understood what she meant by small.

It was mostly a box, a square box with a tarred roof. The grass in front was brown scrub peppered with weeds, the walkway to the tiny porch buckled and the steps were in lousy shape as well. There was no garage, and from the look of the people loitering on the street, he was glad he'd gotten the extra insurance from the rental agency.

He made no comment as he parked. She got her own bag out, and he retrieved his, but as she approached the front door, she seemed hyper-vigilant, checking behind her before she slid the key in.

As he watched one group of kids standing on the nearby corner, they jeered and gestured at a patrol cruiser that didn't bother to slow down.

Becca had been right. It wasn't what he was used to. What bothered him was that Noah was growing up here. Ryder found it hard to believe this was the best Becca could do. She'd been a restaurant manager, and now she was even higher up the ladder. Surely she could have found safe housing somewhere.

Inside wasn't nearly as chilly as the weather outside, which felt more like spring than autumn. The place was neat and orderly. The furniture didn't match, but there was a decent-looking couch, a Noah-sized chair and a box of toys.

There was no separate dining room. Just a plain kitchen with an old stove, a sink, a refrigerator that rumbled and one long counter where she'd have to do everything. The cupboards looked to be pasteboard and needed paint.

"Which one's Noah's room?"

Becca stopped with her hand on the fridge door. "I told you it wasn't much more than a closet. You'll never fit."

"I'll be fine."

She shrugged and nodded at the door to the left of the small bathroom. He noticed there was no tub, just a shower and a sink with a small cupboard underneath.

When he opened the door to Noah's room, he realized she hadn't exaggerated. It was a closet, repurposed with a child's bed, something that wouldn't take Noah very long to outgrow. There were three shelves at the foot of the bed where his clothes were folded.

He closed the door and looked back. "I'll take the couch."

"Suit yourself," she said, sipping a glass of what looked like juice. "I can make coffee if you want. I don't have milk, but I do have sugar."

"Don't bother. It's late. I'm going to call my mom, then try to get some sleep. If Noah is still awake, I'll let you know."

She glanced at the wall clock. "He should be asleep. I'll call in the morning." Her eyes were bloodshot and swollen, and the skin around her nostrils looked in-flamed. The attractive woman he'd grown used to had been replaced by someone years older, and so sad it was as if she'd been crying for weeks.

He'd shed his own tears, but he was far more worried

about the state of his mother. Sitting down on the couch, the first thing he saw on the weird patchwork coffee table were pamphlets for two different women's shelters and a rehab center. He picked them up, and there were notes to Amy, handwritten, with words of encouragement and love. No censure, no blackmail. Just support.

He tossed them back on the table.

Becca walked up to the couch, her travel bag in her hand. "There's juice and water in the fridge. If you want something to eat, help yourself. There's linen under the sink in the bathroom. Good night."

With that, she walked into the only bedroom and closed the door sharply behind her.

He just sat there, dreading making the call he needed to, listening to sirens near and distant, hip-hop blaring from the streets as cars drove by, helicopters, airplanes. It was as if he'd landed on some other planet.

When he finally pulled out his phone, he heard Becca talking to someone. But by the time he dialed, all he heard was sobbing.

He didn't finish the call. Went to the bathroom, got a sheet and the world's flattest pillow and brought them back to the couch after using the facilities.

He'd stay in his jeans and shirt. Debated keeping his boots on, but the couch didn't look as if it could take the wear.

Then he took a deep breath and dialed home.

ISABELLA'S QUICK KNOCK at the door came early, but Becca was up. She'd barely slept, and now she could hardly see through her swollen eyes. Everything in her world was dark and miserable and she was so frightened she couldn't think straight.

Somehow, she'd managed to shower and dress. It was

hard not to notice that Ryder had been sleeping on the couch with the pillow over his head. Probably all the noise. It was easy to forget about how loud it was in the city.

Now she needed coffee, and a cold compress on her eyes. Too bad if it woke up Ryder. He'd made little to no effort to consider her anything but the villain, and while she couldn't blame him, between his anger and her worries over Noah's future, she was an utter wreck.

Isabella had already finished making the coffee when Becca made it to the kitchen. She quickly pulled Becca into a hug.

She couldn't start crying again. She'd called Isabella last night and filled her in on what had happened. Now she was so choked up she could barely breathe.

Finally, Isabella pulled back but still held on to Becca's arms. "How are you?" she whispered.

"Worse than I look."

"I know this has to be so hard for you. Please, just remember, Amy chose her own path. You did everything you could possibly do. I just hope that *bastardo* rots in hell forever. Now, other than coffee, what do you need?"

"Me? Nothing. I'll be going back this afternoon, flying all night, really. We have to change planes twice, but I don't care. I need to get back to Noah. And then, I'm not sure when we'll come home." She sniffed, lowered her gaze so she wasn't looking into Isabella's eyes. "He loves it on the ranch so much. He'll hate coming home."

"So, you've made up your mind. Good. Don't worry about Noah, he'll be happy wherever you are. You know that's true. He loves you more than anyone in the world. Thank God we don't have to worry about Derek looking for you anymore."

The thing was, Becca really hadn't made up her mind. She'd thought she had, and she would've left Noah in

Blackfoot Falls if she'd been asked to testify. But all night long, she'd thought about Noah living on the ranch. No Aunt Amy. No Señora Rios. No Mommy. He'd be so scared. So lost. He'd hate her for leaving him. "I just wish..."

Isabella pulled her close again. The woman only came up to Becca's shoulders, but she was strong. In so many ways. What she couldn't do was help Becca stop crying. Amy was gone. Really gone.

Footsteps fell behind her, but Isabella didn't release her hold. Just moved the two of them closer to the table. She heard Ryder open the cabinet, put a cup down, pour his coffee.

Becca hoped he hadn't heard that last comment. It wasn't too revealing but it could raise some questions. Stepping back, giving Isabella the best smile she could manage, she introduced her to Ryder.

"Nice to meet you," he said, then went around the table, back to the couch and sat.

He looked terrible, which was only fair.

"So, you talked to your boss?" Isabella asked.

Becca got her own coffee, then poured another for her friend. "Yes. He was a little impatient with me, but I told him I needed another week. He wants me back as quickly as possible. I honestly thought he would fire me."

"He understands what it means to have emergencies."

"I suppose," she said, then took a sip of coffee. It was bitter. She'd forgotten to add her usual teaspoon of sugar. "I can't afford to be any longer than that." She sipped again, the hell with sugar. "It feels unreal that I spoke to him yesterday from my grandparents' house. It's all unreal."

Isabella frowned. "This isn't a paid leave? You've worked there for years."

"No. I used up my vacation when Noah was sick, and since then I've accrued only a couple days." Her throat got tight again, especially when she noticed that Ryder had quietly come back into the kitchen, behind her and was about to get another cup of coffee.

"You know, I should call Noah right now," Becca said, feeling as helpless and vulnerable as a baby. "He's probably wondering what happened to me."

She had to get out of there, at least for a few minutes, although she didn't like leaving Isabella alone with Ryder. Not that Isabella would say anything indiscreet.

"Go call," Isabella said. "I'll make more coffee."

She hurried away, closed the door behind her, but there was no way she was calling Noah. Not when she was falling apart.

"I'M SORRY FOR your loss," Isabella said. "I knew Amy, too, and I'll miss her. She was a sweet girl and didn't deserve what happened to her."

Ryder jerked a little as he spun around but didn't lose any of his coffee. Isabella was an older woman, her dark hair threaded with gray. She clearly cared a lot for Becca and Noah. "Thank you." He started to head for the safety of the couch again but hesitated. "How long have you known them?"

"Becca and Amy?"

"Becca and Noah."

She smiled. "From the day he was born. It's been my true joy to help with Noah. He's such a bright boy. So full of questions and mischief."

A loud pop from the street made him jerk again. It could've been a backfire and not a gunshot, but he wouldn't count on it. He shook his head. "Becca shouldn't be living here. Especially with Noah. I don't understand why she would risk him in this environment."

Isabella's smile disappeared. "You do know that Los Angeles is expensive. One of the most expensive cities to live."

"No, I get that. But maybe if they lived farther away, it would be safer. If she's worried about her car, I know there's public transportation. She already goes to work on a bus. I mean, Noah's safety is the most important thing. He's just four. He must go out sometimes, and the gangs—"

"Mr. Mitchell, Becca always puts Noah's safety first. Always."

She stepped closer to him, and it was tempting to back up. She looked as fierce as any mother protecting her child.

"You have no idea what she's gone through to take care of that boy. What she's sacrificed. He has everything he needs. And me to take care of him when she's at work. It might be a poor neighborhood, but not everyone who lives here is a gang member. Becca hasn't had a life of her own since the day he was born. She doesn't spend a penny on herself."

He shrugged, not terribly moved. "Isn't that what a mother's supposed to do? Bullets don't discriminate. They go through walls. Couches. Doors."

With her lips tightly pressed together, Isabella's eyes were blazing but she took a moment. "I know you're grieving, Mr. Mitchell. I understand what loss can do to a person. But you'd better think twice before you take out your anger on Becca because you also don't know what she did to help your sister. Amy couldn't have had a better friend. You think Becca wanted to live here, work in a restaurant all day? Think again."

Ryder looked out the small kitchen window, into the crumbling wall that separated the neighbor's house from this one. "I'm sorry I offended you. It's just… LA of all places. I can't imagine what it was like for those two at eighteen. They were kids from rural Montana. Why did they stay here when they could have been back home? Blackfoot Falls isn't some armpit. It was a great place to grow up. To live."

"This was always Amy's dream. Surely you know that. She wanted the city lights, to be invited to all the big parties, maybe act. She tried. It's hard to let go of childhood dreams."

Ryder closed his eyes, remembering what his mother had told him about Amy. And the truth was, he already knew it had all been her idea, not Becca's. What didn't make sense was why Becca wouldn't have said something.

He sighed. Why the hell was he so anxious to blame everything on Becca?

His gut clenched. It wasn't a complete mystery. Every time he tried not to think about Amy, his thoughts bounced to his marriage, to his mom and how he'd failed in so many ways. Expanding the ranch seemed to be the only thing he'd been able to do right. But at what cost? Becca, and her hyper-sense of responsibility, her loyalty to Amy and of course Noah, made him question too many things about himself.

Isabella walked to the door, but she didn't open it. She made sure she was looking straight at Ryder first. "Would I like to see Becca and Noah living in a better neighborhood? Of course. But for what it's worth, I've raised three children not far from here. An obstetrician, a wonderful wife and mother and a proud Marine."

Ryder nodded, regretting his words. "I don't doubt it. Thank you for telling me."

She bowed her head graciously and left him to his thoughts. Which centered directly on Becca and Noah. Who, dammit, didn't belong here.

They shouldn't come back to Los Angeles, and they wouldn't. Not if he could help it.

Chapter Sixteen

"I promise, sweetie, we'll be home really soon."

"Did you miss me?"

"So much," Becca said, hoping her voice didn't sound as weak as she felt. The flights from LA to Kalispell had been exhausting. They'd crisscrossed half the country, and it had been tense and awkward and she'd almost ordered alcohol in hopes that she would sleep. But instead, she'd pretended to read magazines while Ryder drank coffee after coffee.

At least they were on the road home now, in his familiar truck, and Noah was waiting for her at the other end. One bright light in a world of dark gray.

"I have a hug to give you from Señora Rios," Becca told him over the phone. "She misses you a lot."

"Does she know I saw cows? And horses?"

"Yep. And she also knows you picked out the Christmas tree."

"I know! But I wanted to tell her."

"You can tell her when you see her. She'll like hearing about it from you."

"Did you tell Aunt Amy?"

Becca's throat closed and she pressed her palm to her eyes to stop the sudden flood of tears.

"Mommy?"

She couldn't. It was as if a dam had broken.

"Put him on speaker," Ryder said. "I have something to ask him."

She ended up just putting the phone in his hand, and he put it on speaker. "Hey, buddy, what are you doing up so late?"

"'Cause Mommy's coming home. Then I have to go straight to bed."

"Have you been taking care of Aunt Gail?"

"Me and Uncle Wiley have. We cooked her dinner last night."

"Really?"

"I don't think she likes hot dogs and beans, though."

"I'll bet she loved that you cooked them."

"I got to eat almost two hot dogs by myself."

"Wow. You're getting big. Now, you need to go get ready for bed because we're going to be there in a few minutes. Say bye to Mommy, real loud so she can hear you."

"Bye, Mommy!"

"Bye, sweetie," she said, although she had no idea if he heard her through her snuffling.

Ryder handed her back the phone, and she put it in her pocket. "I'm sorry. I promise I'll pull myself together before we get home. I'm not even family, but I can't help—"

"Hey," he said, his tone low and calm. "Amy was as much your sister as mine. You knew her better. And at least you tried to get her help."

A sob wracked Becca's body, and it was as if she hadn't grieved at all. The tears wouldn't stop. She was doubled over, the seat belt cutting into her neck, but she couldn't stop. She might never stop.

When Ryder stroked a hand down her hair, she realized the truck had pulled over to the side of the highway.

He released her seat belt and eased her into his arms, holding her tight.

Still stroking her hair, he didn't try to shush her but whispered softly that it was okay. "I'm sorry for all the grief I gave you. I know you didn't deserve it. Detective Richardson was absolutely right. You were a good friend. You did your best."

Instead of making her feel better, his kindness made her sink even lower, but after using every bit of fortitude she had, she managed to stuff the feelings down. "It's a terrible time for everyone," she said, sounding as if she'd forgotten how to speak. "We all say things we regret."

He nodded, his stubbled chin scratching against the side of her cheek. She hadn't realized he'd gotten that close. He kept petting her, holding her, and it seemed as if the world had slowed. It was a gift, being in his arms. All she wanted to do was let go, rest her head on his chest until she fell asleep. Forget everything but how he made her feel right this second.

But of course, she couldn't. There was a wall between them, no matter how tight his arms. The big lie was still there, and the second she told him, he'd hate her so much worse than he had. There would be no comfort offered. Ever again.

And then she'd lose the one person who made her want to get up every morning. Who made it all right that Amy had tricked her into leaving her future behind. Noah had become her reason. Her life. She'd wither and die without him.

But he'd never been hers to keep.

Lifting her head up and leaning away from Ryder, she dug another tissue out of her purse. It didn't help all that much, but at least she'd sobered enough that she could respond appropriately. "Thank you. But we really do need to get home. Noah's up so late, and I'm anxious to see how your mother's doing."

"Sure you're all right?"

A single nod was all she could give him, but after another squeeze of her hand, he got them back onto the highway.

Time blurred and then they were pulling up in front of the house. The moment Ryder parked, the front door opened, and there was Gail, holding Noah's hand. He was in his pajamas and had on a thick robe, one Gail must have bought for him. The slippers were still his Disney *Cars* red ones that he loved so much.

Gail, though, was leaning heavily on her cane. It could have been the overhead light, but she looked older than before they'd left. Yet she still managed a strained smile.

Becca jumped out of the car and rushed to hug Noah—so hard he whimpered.

"Mommy, too tight."

"Sorry, baby. I just missed you so much." She held him at arm's length so they could look at each other, and then she noticed that the whole front of the house was strung with lights. "What's all this?"

"Christmas!" Noah said, very loudly. "Me and Uncle Wiley did it all."

"I'll bet you did," she said, noticing also that Uncle Wiley looked about ready to drop from exhaustion. But he stood behind Gail, a firm hand on her shoulder.

Becca and Noah led the way inside, where she discovered that the tree had been put in the bucket, and the lowest branches had been decorated in a very Noah sort of way. The whole living room was filled with little snowmen and angels and different Santas. It all seemed too cheerful. Enough of a distraction, Becca supposed, for the forty-eight hours they'd been gone.

"I made coffee, and I've got leftover beef stew if you're hungry." Gail made a move toward the kitchen, but before she could get far, Ryder stopped her and gave her a hug that was so loving Becca had to leave the room. At least she had the excuse of putting Noah to bed.

Of course he didn't want to sleep, not with so much excitement. But she let him tell her all the details of the decorating and cooking and hanging lights with Uncle Wiley.

"Did you miss home? Because Señora Rios misses you a lot."

Noah thought a few seconds. "I miss her, too, but I like being here with Aunt Gail and Uncle Wiley and Uncle Ryder and the horses better."

Her heart sank, and it was hell to hide it, but she did. For him. Of course he'd say that. It was only natural. They lived in a horrid tiny house, with gunshots and sirens and danger. She was gone so often for work, and here, he was loved every day by so many people, and he was free to run and play and explore.

Noah tugged on her arm. "I have a secret."

"You do?"

He nodded, his eyelids starting to droop.

She leaned down close.

"I heard Aunt Gail and Uncle Wiley, and they said Uncle Ryder's getting me a pony."

Becca could barely breathe. Ryder knew they had to leave. She had no choice. Her job. Her house. Her bills. Her life. It would be cruel to get Noah a pony when they'd have to leave it behind.

Inhaling sharply, she sat up. Noah was having trouble keeping his eyes open. "We'll talk about that later," she said, brushing his hair off his forehead.

He almost nodded, but she knew he was down for the

night. She still kissed his cheek and told him she loved him, and even though all she wanted to do was crawl in next to him, she couldn't.

Especially after realizing she'd already made up her mind to take Noah home. It hadn't been a conscious decision…but she knew in her heart Noah belonged with her. That didn't mean she would keep the Mitchells out of his life. They just couldn't know everything.

She couldn't face the consequences of that train of thought tonight, not when she was so exhausted. But she would have to speak to Ryder about the pony. Perhaps Noah had misunderstood. At least, she hoped so.

"IT JUST DOESN'T seem possible."

Ryder didn't even blink when his mother looked at him as if he was supposed to have the answers. That he could fix this if he really tried. The knowledge that he was helpless nearly crippled him, but the truth was, all he could do was be there. Just like he'd done when his father had died.

So useless.

"I know it's unreal," he said. They were in the kitchen. Both their coffees left untouched. His mother's eyes were puffy and rimmed with red, her silent pleas heartbreaking. He had no idea what to say to her. Tell the truth? Lie? Make something up so she could get some sleep? If he had the words, he'd use them, but he had nothing to offer.

"Becca must have felt so terrible, not being there for her."

"She had to make sure Noah was safe. She did the right thing, Mom." He covered her hand with his own. "But I saw how hard she tried to get Amy help. She tried to talk her into going to rehab or a shelter. She offered to bring her home, but Amy was more stubborn than I ever realized. You were right."

His mother winced. "I wanted to be wrong. I should have gone to see her. I could have traveled, even after your father died. But I should have gone long before that."

"No. That was supposed to be my job. I'm your son. I should have been there for my baby sister. I could have made her come back." That he'd actually been in LA on business and he'd let her brush him off had taken a bite out of him on the last connecting flight home. It was still eating at him. He'd had a hell of a lot of nerve tearing into Becca.

"No, don't. Don't. We all failed her. Probably because we all thought she could conquer anything. She was so headstrong. So determined."

Ryder nodded, even though he didn't like her blaming herself. He'd talked to Amy when she was obviously drunk. High. But the minute he'd put down the phone, he'd gone right back to ignoring the problem. He'd shaken his head. Then gone on with his life.

"So, this man, this evil man. He's dead now, and he won't have to pay for hurting my child?"

Ryder smiled. "He didn't get away with anything. He got what he deserved, and once the police finish their investigation, the record will be set straight. She tried to get away from him. But he caught her. At least she did try in the end."

"You know that?"

"She went to see Becca. She even got Noah a toy and gave Becca some money. Amy had a plan. She was going to run away. Once she was safe, she was supposed to let Becca know where she was."

"But he caught her."

Ryder nodded. Noticed the trembling again. According to Wiley, she'd been doing it often. Trembling all over, her face getting red. "I think we should go see Dr. Heaton tomorrow."

"No, I'm not going. Anyway, you have that meeting in Evergreen."

He'd completely forgotten. "I'll put off the meeting. You're more important."

"Listen, I'm a grown woman and I'm telling you I don't need to see the doctor. All that's wrong with me is heartache and fatigue."

Ryder leaned back in his chair. It would have felt better to walk around, move his muscles, after all the time he'd spent in cars and planes. But he wasn't getting up except to help her to bed. "I'm sorry I left you to watch Noah. I should have realized he'd wear you out. I know what that kid's like. He's too much for you."

She laughed. "It was the other way around. Noah was an angel. He tried to help me do everything—decorate, cook. He told me stories about the moon and about the truck that Amy got him. I'm surprised he lasted so late tonight. I don't know what I would have done without him."

"So he distracted you, huh?"

"Honestly, he was good for me. I didn't want him to see me so sad. For him, I smiled. I hung up ornaments. He chose where to put every single Christmas trinket we have. They're not just out here. You obviously haven't been to your room yet."

"No, I haven't. What did he put in yours?"

She looked a little better when she talked about Noah. "Two toy cars. They're his favorite ones. And remember that old Christmas tree blanket we had?"

"The one we used to put around the base of the tree?"

She nodded. "He found it, and insisted I needed it for my blanket, so I wouldn't shiver so much."

Why in hell did Becca keep insisting she needed to go back to California? She didn't have anything to go back to. Isabella was nice, but now that Amy…

It didn't make sense for Becca to stay in LA. She'd even told the detective that she and Amy had talked about how they wished they'd never left Blackfoot Falls. Now, she was talking about her work as if it was something special. From what she'd told him, she couldn't be making any kind of decent money.

Besides, the only reason she was so happy to have that job was because it let her see Noah more. If she stayed in Blackfoot Falls, it would be cheaper to live, no long commutes…she'd see him all the time.

And it would mean the world to his mother. She wasn't half as old as she looked, or as feeble. All that had come about after his dad died. Gail had always been as strong as an ox. Until she'd lost a daughter and a husband, and her son had ended up childless and divorced.

Ryder needed to figure out a way to convince Becca to stay. That was as clear as the sadness in his mom's eyes. There had to be something for her here that would be more satisfying than being stuck in an office.

Even if he had to create a job and hire her himself, it would be worth it. Everyone would be happier. Including him.

Hell, especially him. Despite all the crap he'd given her, all the nasty accusations—some of which he had truly believed, and which could be the very thing that ended up chasing her away—it was hard to think back to how things were before she'd returned.

Noah might be his mom's tonic but Becca was Ryder's.

Grief had temporarily turned him into a real bastard, and he hoped she could forgive him. Because it wasn't grief making him feel the way he did about her. It might not be love yet, but…

"You know what we'll have to do?"

"What?" His mother looked at him with such indulgence. Even she knew he had no answer. Not that he would tell her outright what he was thinking. There was always a chance he wouldn't be able to sway Becca, although he'd give it everything he had.

"We'll just have to think of a way to keep them here. Right?"

She patted his hand and reached for her cane. "Right," she said. "But tonight, I'm going to go to bed."

"Let me walk you," he said, rising as she stood.

"No, go get some sleep yourself. That meeting of yours is early, and you look terrible."

"Thanks."

"I love you, son. Thank you for all you're doing for us."

He couldn't even speak after that. All he'd done was so far shy of what he should have. Instead, he watched her make her way down the hall, to the master bedroom at the end.

But just when he was about to head up himself, he caught Becca standing midway down the stairs. He had no idea how long she'd been there, or what she'd heard. But she didn't look happy.

Chapter Seventeen

It was almost 10:00 a.m. when Becca opened her eyes. She hadn't slept that late in ages. As tired as she'd been last night, she'd lain awake for hours, worrying about Gail, thinking about Amy and how Becca had let her down.

This situation with Noah had to be resolved. Soon. Because all the flip-flopping was killing her. Eating away at her soul.

She'd ended up changing her mind again, decided she definitely would tell them, no matter the consequences. But then she'd panicked. Literally. It had felt as if she was having a heart attack, and she couldn't breathe, and the walls were closing in on her. It was horrible, and it had happened twice last night.

The problem was, she couldn't imagine a life without Noah. He'd been hers from the moment of his birth. Amy had basically given him to Becca. In her heart, in her every decision and action, she'd been living for Noah. She hadn't hesitated for a second to use all her meager savings to take care of his needs. Thank goodness for charity shops. They'd been her source for everything from clothing to his crib to his car seat. The only new toys he'd ever gotten were gifts from Amy.

But Gail and Ryder would want to know why she hadn't called them to take over.

She'd never planned on telling them about Amy's lies about her family, and now that Amy was dead, Becca would rather die herself than ambush Gail, or Ryder, with something so horrible.

But if given the chance to go back to the beginning, to Noah's birth, would she have done things differently, even knowing how it would end?

She wasn't sure. She'd like to think she would, but the largest part of her identity was being Noah's mommy.

Pushing herself up, she focused on making her bed, taking a shower, getting dressed. Noah had clearly been up for a while, and for all she knew, he was out in the barn or riding on the ATV with Wiley.

In the kitchen, she was stunned to see Gail at the stove making what looked like a pot of soup. It was a good sign, Becca thought as she poured herself a mug of coffee and looked out the garden window.

Noah was at the corral, sitting with Wiley on the rail, watching Bear work with a horse. Her son wore a Western shirt she didn't recognize. And a Noah-sized Stetson.

Evidently, Gail had bought him more than just the robe. He was turning into a regular cowpoke, which made Becca's stomach clench. Yet another blow to her taking him back to LA. She didn't think the Mitchells were doing it maliciously, but it felt like a plot to win Noah over to their side.

She was quite certain that mission had already been accomplished.

The breath left her chest, and the squeezing started. She had to put her hand on the counter to keep herself steady.

Gail got herself a cup of coffee and sat down at the kitchen table. "Will you come sit with me for a minute?"

Becca nodded, topped off her cup, then joined Noah's grandmother. Not a smart thought. It made her wince, and when she looked at Gail again, Gail was touching her eyes.

"I know I look terrible," she said, her voice strained.

"I'm sure I don't look any better," Becca replied, "but I'm so glad to see you up and about."

"Oh, I'm fine. Maybe still in a bit of shock, but aren't we all?" She paused. "I'd like to ask you some questions about Amy, if you can bear it. If not, I understand."

"Ask me whatever you need to," Becca said, grasping Gail's trembling hand.

"I don't know much about Amy's life in California. I have a feeling that most of what she told me wasn't exactly true."

Becca wanted to curl up and weep, but she had to be there for Gail. It was the very least she could do. "We thought it would be far more glamorous than it turned out to be. Remember that school field trip we took to Bozeman? We were all excited to go to the Museum of the Rockies?"

"And got in trouble for leaving the motel in the middle of the night."

"Yes, that's true."

"Amy's idea," Gail said with a sigh.

Becca closed her eyes for a moment, a quick flash of the Amy she'd known then making her smile. "She was quite the troublemaker."

"And you went along with every crazy plan."

"Not every plan."

"But you did go to LA with her. I always wondered why."

There was no way in the world she'd admit to Gail the real reason behind her decision to leave. It might actually kill her to know how Amy had lied so viciously about the two men Gail loved most in the world. "I admit, she made it sound like something wonderful. She was so sure we'd end up in Hollywood, hobnobbing with all the celebrities. And maybe even getting into the movie business herself." Becca shrugged. "We were kids."

"Early on, she told me something about getting into modeling. Was that true?"

"Partly. She did get that one job for a local chain store, but that was pretty much it. She was so proud. Certain it would lead to better things."

"It was after that she lost hope, didn't she?"

"I'm not sure." Becca paused to take a sip from her mug. "She was always broke and some guy talked her into taking a short course in bartending. It was great in the beginning. She was good at it, and she started out with a very upscale bar. Met a few Hollywood people."

"Meanwhile you were working as a waitress?"

"I had some housekeeping jobs, too. There are so many motels and hotels in LA. It was steady work, and between that, my job at the restaurant and her tips from the bar, we made the rent."

"But then she got into..." Gail couldn't speak. She closed her eyes and Becca got nervous.

"Whatever you're cooking smells wonderful."

Gail pulled a tissue from under her shirt cuff, and pressed it to her eyes for a moment. When she looked at Becca again, she seemed a little better. "It's Ryder's favorite. He loves my chicken and dumplings. I thought you and Noah might like it, too."

"You probably make the dumplings from scratch, right? You don't cut up dough from a can?"

Gail actually laughed. "I never heard of such a thing. Those wouldn't be dumplings. If you like, I'll teach you how to make them."

"That would be great," she said. "I haven't seen Ryder this morning."

"He's off at a business meeting. He almost forgot about it. It's in Evergreen, which isn't all that far away. I just hope he doesn't get lost in work like he did after the divorce. I swear, he nearly worked himself to death buying up land, increasing the herd. He was a man possessed, determined to prove something."

"Prove?"

"I don't know, but that was my impression." Gail patted the table and stood up, her cane at the ready. Before she went back to the stove, she met Becca's gaze. "When he gets back, we'll talk about the memorial service."

Becca jerked a little, the statement caught her so off guard.

"If you don't want to, that's fine, sweetheart, but I've always felt as if you were part of the family. You spent so much time with us, and whether you believe it or not, you were a very good influence on Amy."

"I don't know about that," Becca said, "but I do know you always made me feel welcome, and I appreciate that so much. I'm sorry I didn't keep in touch with you more after the move. I should have."

Gail turned to look out the window. "I imagine you were kept quite busy by a certain curious little boy. What a fine job you've done with him. He's such a caring child. You have no idea how much he's done for me. You know, I used to envy Katie when you girls were teenagers. Amy was so caught up in makeup and boys, but you were levelheaded and down-to-earth. I always figured you'd be the one to give your mom grandchildren, and

Amy… Well, she might have, eventually, but—" Gail shrugged and took out the tissue again.

Becca had to force herself not to run as far and as fast as she could. This was torture. Nothing was okay about any of it, and she was to blame. Yes, Amy was headstrong, but Becca was the one who could have stopped it all. If only she'd known the truth. If only she'd been stronger.

Finally, she managed to say, "Ryder still has a few good years left in him."

Gail's shoulders shook, but then Becca heard her laugh. She hadn't meant it as a joke, but she was grateful that's how it had sounded.

"I suppose he does," she said. "At least that's what I keep telling him." She stirred the soup, then turned back to Becca. "Anyway, I'm so happy to have met Noah. He's been a bright light in my life, even in this short time. I can't help wondering if there's any chance you might consider moving back to Blackfoot Falls?"

The panic response was at the ready, but Becca took charge. "I honestly don't know. I assume Ryder told you about where we live. It's not as bad as he thinks it is. I promise. And my job is a good one, with a lot of growth potential."

Gail nodded slowly. "I hope you know you're welcome to stay with us. Always."

"That's a lovely offer, and I appreciate it with all my heart, but I meant to tell you I decided last night that it would be best for Noah and me to move over to my grandparents' house for a few days before we head back to LA."

Now it was Gail who seemed panicked, her eyes wide and fretful. "When?"

"This afternoon."

Gail leaned heavily on her cane. "But there's no heating or electricity. There's no refrigerator. What could you possibly—?"

Becca stood, walked over to Gail and put grounding hands on her shoulders. "We'll be fine. I've figured it all out." That was a total lie. She'd spoken out of panic, but she stayed the course. "With that wood-burning stove, we'll be all set, and of course, we'll come by as often as you like. But you'll be having a lot of company soon. Half of Blackfoot Falls will be coming to pay their respects. Noah and I would just be in the way."

"No. Not at all. You don't have to leave."

Becca forced a smile. "I promise, we'll be warm and safe, and so close by that you won't even have a chance to miss us. I'll be here whenever you need me, and Noah will be out bothering Wiley and you until you want to wring your hands. But we'll leave you in peace, as well. This is just a difficult time. It'll all work out.

"Now, I'd better go make sure Noah isn't being a nuisance, and then I'll pack our things. We'll come back later to talk about the memorial service." She kissed Gail on the cheek. The weakest apology in the world.

The truth was, she couldn't stay. Not with them, not without waffling over the huge decision she had to make. She was in knots, and she had to have a clear head before she botched things up forever. She had to think. And she couldn't while she had to face this family every minute.

She was being selfish. But they all deserved for her to be rational. Noah deserved her best judgment. After all, he'd be losing the only mother he'd ever known.

And she'd be losing everything.

Chapter Eighteen

The smell of chicken and dumplings welcomed Ryder home just after four o'clock. The meeting at Evergreen had gone on too long, but he'd taken his time checking out the stock, particularly the two breeding bulls. Now that he'd increased the herd, he needed to add two sires to take care of the overflow, and Evergreen Ranch had just what he was looking for.

If nothing else, the meeting had been a great distraction. His thoughts kept wandering, and not just because he was worried about his mother, which only added to his guilt. He kept thinking about Becca and about whether she could ever really forgive him.

Last night, as he'd tried to lose himself in sleep, stray bits of conversation since receiving the news of Amy's death kept drifting back to him.

Hell, it wasn't conversation—it was just him, and his damned self-righteousness, verbally battering Becca, who hadn't deserved any of it. All because he'd felt so powerless. He'd been so blinded by anger and his own guilt that he'd blocked out some of the truly terrible things he'd said to her. Until random memories started coming back to haunt him.

After hanging up his jacket, he found his mother at

the kitchen table sitting by herself. No Becca, no Noah, no Wiley.

"Mom, you okay?"

She looked up and gave him the saddest excuse for a nod.

He sat down next to her. "What happened?"

"It's all right," she said. "I'm sure she has her reasons."

"Who's she?"

"Becca." It sounded as if she'd used the last bit of her energy to utter the name.

"What did she do?"

His mother looked at him, and he thought about calling Doc Heaton whether she wanted to see him or not. "She and Noah have moved over to her grandparents' place."

"What? That doesn't make any sense."

"I didn't think so either, but she seemed determined."

"Determined?" he repeated, confused. "To leave you here alone?"

"I'm hardly alone, Ryder." She sighed. "You must be hungry. Let me get you some dinner."

"I want to understand why Becca left." He got a glass from the cabinet and filled it with water. "Did she give you a reason?"

"Because people will be coming by to offer their condolences. And that I need time to rest. That Noah would wear me out."

"Well, there must be some kind of misunderstanding. She wouldn't just pick up and go like that." He thought about her standing on the stairs last night and that tense look on her face. "Did you mention that we were going to discuss the memorial service?"

Gail nodded. "I don't know why, but I think that might be why she decided to leave. I don't think she wants to help with that."

"She doesn't want—"

"It's fine. It's her choice. I told her she didn't have to."

Ryder set the water in front of her, then paced the length of the kitchen. He looked out the window to see if anyone was in the corral but all he saw was Otis walking toward the bunkhouse. "This is crazy. Something's wrong with this picture. She's at her grandparents' house now?"

"I think so. Her car is gone, didn't you notice?"

"I didn't give it any thought. How could she just leave?"

"We have no right to keep them here, Ryder."

"No, but we can sure as hell tell her that house doesn't belong to her family anymore."

"You can't do that," she said, sighing. "Wiley has been checking on me all day, and I invited him to come by for dinner. Don't get worked up about Becca. She's not running away. She probably just needs some time alone."

He didn't understand. Becca wouldn't take Noah to a house with… "No electricity, no heat, no fridge. How are they going manage? She's got a four-year-old with her."

"There's wood and a stove that will keep them both warm."

He knew that wouldn't be enough, but the last thing he wanted was to make his mom more upset.

"I'll go tell Wiley to come over while I check on them," he said.

"If you're just going to bother Becca, I don't think you should. She's grieving."

"I won't be long. Why don't I make you a cup of tea before I go?"

"You're grieving, too, Ryder. You need time to grieve, just as Becca needs room to get over her loss. I know you care about her. And Noah. It's obvious. Leave it be for tonight."

He turned away, knowing his mother was right. "I'm attracted to her. That's different. But that's not what's important now. I just want to make sure she understands she's still welcome here."

"I don't want to argue. Please."

"I'm sorry, I didn't mean to upset you. I'll be back soon."

He left the kitchen before she had a chance to say another word, and he barely remembered to grab his jacket.

WHEN HE GOT to the old ranch house seven minutes later, he parked the truck behind the big oak about thirty feet from the door and sat for a minute, just taking some deep breaths. He wasn't going to go in there accusing Becca of running out on them. He'd ask her, calmly, why she'd left.

When he was ready, he got out, closed the door as quietly as possible, then headed toward the house. As he got close, something caught his eye inside. The curtains were all the way open and he could see clear into the kitchen.

Becca was sweeping like it was a competition. He could tell she'd cleaned off the counters and had been dusting. And that tears were streaming down her face.

"Well, shit." His mother's words came back to him, clearer this time. Becca was grieving for her friend. He still didn't like her being without the basic necessities, but he needed to give her space. Respect her decision. They could talk tomorrow.

"Uncle Ryder?"

He spun around at Noah's voice. The boy stood to the side of the small porch, looking confused.

"Hey, Noah."

"How come you didn't come in?"

The door swung open and Becca's call for her son was

cut off. She stared at Ryder, more panicked than anything, wiping furiously at her tear-streaked face.

"We're having a new 'venture. Kinda like camping. But inside."

Ryder shifted his attention to Noah, although he only had a vague idea of what the boy had said. "Sounds exciting." His gaze moved quickly back to Becca. She was in jeans and a T-shirt, and it was too cold for that. At least Noah had his jacket on. "Look, I just came by to see if you needed anything. I have a pretty big cooler I could bring over…you could use it to keep milk, or whatever."

The look she gave him was far too wary. "Um, thanks. We have a small one, so we're fine. It's just for a few days." She sniffed quietly. "Oh, you know what, we left a few things, toys mostly, in the guest room. Please tell your mom I'll be by tomorrow to pick them up and straighten the room."

"Is this because of the plans to talk about the service—?"

"What? No." She glanced at Noah, who was still staring at Ryder. "I'll come by later. I'm sorry, I forgot that we were supposed to make…plans…and…"

Her lips were quivering and more tears fell. He felt rooted to the pathway. When her head bowed, he rushed forward, pulling her into his arms. "God, you're freezing," he whispered. "We should get you inside."

She shook her head, but he wasn't sure what she was trying to say no to, so he just took the initiative and pulled her back into the house. Becca clung to his every move, trying like a trooper to stop weeping, but all she managed was some sniffles and stutters.

"What's wrong, Mommy?"

"Come on inside, Noah," Ryder said. When he heard the front door close, he leaned back and held her tighter. "Mommy's okay. It's me. I've been an idiot." He lowered his voice so his words would only reach her ears. "I knew you were grieving, but I didn't give you any space to do that. I was so concerned with my own confusion, I left you out to dry, didn't I?"

That seemed to make her worse. She sobbed like a child, and all he could do was hold her. Stroke her hair, brush a kiss across her cheek. He wanted to do a lot more. "You're a working single mom and you need your job and your life back. None of this is fair. Not any of it. Especially when you tried so hard to help Amy."

Her hand went between her own chest and his, and he let his grip loosen. She probably couldn't breathe. She gave Noah a shaky smile.

"You want me to get you a tissue?"

She shook her head and walked over to the counter, where she had a roll of toilet paper sitting by the sink. She tore off a piece and used it to wipe her nose.

"Listen, I don't know if this is the right time, but have you given any thought to just, you know, moving here? Back to Blackfoot Falls, I mean. It would be a lot cheaper and safer than LA, and you'd have a lot of help with Noah."

Becca stared at him, eyes misty. Her brow furrowed and she sniffed hard. "I admit, it's crossed my mind, but now that I've got that promotion, things will be better for Noah and me. Not just more pay, but good health insurance and good hours and, well, I can't imagine finding something like that out here."

"That promotion is great, but in R & D for a new chain of steakhouses, won't that mean some travel?"

"Yes, but only day trips, and I have Isabella. Sometimes she gets tied up, but her daughter pitches in."

"Is there a target date for the next restaurant to become operational?"

"In about ten months."

He knew he was pressing hard, and he didn't want to upset her too much, but he had to strike when the iron was hot. "That'll mean a huge time commitment. I assume. How far is it from your house?"

She shook her head, but it was clear he needed to back off. She would more than likely follow his thought…that if the location was a couple of hours away, the commute would be a nightmare. But the last thing he wanted was for her to feel foolish or naive or that he was trying to manipulate her. Which he was, for more reasons than he even understood.

He couldn't help but wonder again why her mother hadn't told her about the place being sold. Did Becca have any family she could count on? She sure never talked about them. After her grandparents had passed, probably all she'd had was Amy and Noah.

"Okay," he said. "I confess, I'm trying too hard. But the truth is, I'd like to continue getting to know you. It would be a lot easier if I didn't have to fly to LA to do it."

A cynical smile curved her lips. "With all the work you have? I thought you were trying to build the biggest ranch in Montana."

Yeah, while he'd ignored his responsibilities as a son and brother. He took her hand, and thankfully, she didn't shake him off. "My mother thinks I'm overcompensating for the divorce, but she's wrong."

Becca looked down.

"I figured she'd said something," Ryder admitted.

"I didn't say that."

Ryder smiled. "I'm going to tell you something even she doesn't know. Leanne and I had been trying to have a baby. We waited—no, *I* waited too long to look into getting some medical help, and by then, we both knew it was too late. The marriage was strained. I screwed up. I suppose I should be grateful we didn't drag an innocent child into it. Because I really wanted a family. Still do."

Becca's breath stuttered. She went perfectly still.

"I understand you're protective of Noah. It's one of the things I admire most about you. But there's so much more to you." He wanted to kiss her, hold on so tight she couldn't leave him. But even though Noah was playing with his truck, he was still shooting looks at them. "You already know my mom considers you like another daughter. And I think in her heart she's already adopted Noah."

Becca looked over at her son, who was sitting on the floor close to the heat of the wood stove. Tears started again.

Ryder wasn't sure whether he'd accomplished what he'd set out to do or if he should feel like an utter heel.

She pushed away and moved over to Noah, scooping him up into her arms. It was as if Ryder had disappeared. Well, guess he *had* been a heel. Or perhaps she'd just realized what kind of man he really was.

BECCA WATCHED RYDER'S truck disappear from view, taking a big chunk of her heart along with him. Despite everything that had happened, she still felt that pull toward him. How easy she could believe that being in his arms again would make everything all right.

How utterly foolish. This wasn't like her. Was it? She hugged Noah tighter. All she wanted to do was take him and make a run for it. She didn't give a damn where they went. She'd just drive until the car broke down and they'd start again. She had a little money set aside, and she could always get a job as a waitress.

She couldn't take this. Ryder talking about wanting a child. Becca wanted that, too. So much. Noah could have a brother or sister. And Ryder would be a good dad. A steady, loving husband. But with all the lies and mistakes she'd made since day one, Ryder would never trust her again. And she wouldn't blame him.

She rocked Noah like she used to when he wouldn't stop crying as an infant, even though it was she who needed the comforting.

She hated who she'd become. Not Noah's mother—that was probably the best thing she would ever do—but that she'd hidden behind her own selfishness when it was clear Noah needed to stay. He loved it here, and he'd have a whole new kind of world to grow up into the amazing man he deserved to be. Ryder would be an amazing—

She couldn't finish the thought without crying again and scaring Noah.

As much as she'd like to think she could give him everything, she couldn't. A huge part of her would die, but she knew what her decision had to be. Tomorrow she would talk to Gail and Ryder, tell them everything, even though they probably would never forgive her.

Only one thing was important. The son of her heart.

Chapter Nineteen

Ryder parked at the ranch and sat in his truck for a minute, trying to work himself into a better mood. It wasn't easy. He felt unsettled, knowing he'd gone too far with Becca. Why had he admitted his part in destroying his marriage? Wasn't it enough that he was feeling guilty over his failures? He'd been discovering some painful truths about himself, and he was willing to own it and change. He was.

Damn, it was so much easier just to work. To focus his energy on the ranch and get so exhausted all he did was fall into bed at the end of the day. But that wasn't the answer. The ranch was no substitute for family. Nothing was. He thought about his father, and how he would have handled the situation.

Dad would have made sure Mom was okay. Moved heaven and earth to help in any way he could. He would have blamed himself for not taking care of Amy right, but he'd have kept that to himself. He would have made sure the cattle were taken care of, the bills were paid, and a nice eulogy that brought out the best of his daughter was in the town paper.

There was Ryder's plan of action, straight down the line. Except for that little complication that was Becca. And Noah. It was true, he did have feelings for Becca.

Strong feelings. He knew it was early, with too much happening, but he'd never felt this kind of a connection with Leanne. And now? The best he could do was give her time.

After a deep breath, he went inside to find Wiley and his mother in the living room. Ryder wasn't hungry, but he'd suck it up and have dinner. That would occupy the three of them for a while.

"How is she?" Gail asked.

Before he responded, he remembered that little smile he'd seen when he'd told Becca he'd like to get to know her better, and that made things easier. "I think you were right. She needs some time, some space to make peace with what's happened. And she's got the stove heating up the house. Noah is happy, he thinks it's a new adventure."

She nodded, almost smiled.

Ryder sat down across from the couch. "I'll give her a couple of hours, then I'll pack up a picnic supper for her and Noah. Make sure they don't miss out on the chicken and dumplings. I thought I'd take a cooler, too, with some milk and some breakfast things. And don't worry, I won't stay long pestering her."

His mom smiled then. "That would be nice. What about the generator we have in the workshop? Maybe then she could make them some hot oatmeal. She could have coffee in the morning. You know she doesn't do well before her first cup."

That made Ryder smile. Mom was sure right about that. "I'll see about it, but I'm hoping she comes back too soon to need a generator."

Gail nodded, and Wiley squeezed her hand. Guess the two of them had made some inroads together. Ryder still wasn't sure if there was more than friendship, and it didn't matter. Wiley had been a champ when it came to helping out, in all manner of ways.

"I suppose we'll talk about the memorial service tomorrow." Gail's voice hitched on the last word.

"I think that's best. Becca said she left some things in their room. Before I forget, I'm going to put them in the back of the truck. Then I could really use a shower." He stood. "Anything I can get you?"

"No, thank you. Wiley's been reminding me of all the mischief Amy used to get into when she was a little girl. She was something else..."

Ryder kissed her on the cheek, squeezed Wiley's shoulder, then went upstairs, past his room. The bedroom where Becca and Noah had stayed wasn't nearly as neat as it usually was. A bag was on the floor, and there were a couple of small cars, a box of crayons and several of Noah's drawings halfway under the bed. Another car was on the nightstand.

He thought about putting it in the bag, maybe collecting the ones Noah had left in Ryder's bedroom, but he didn't want it to seem like he'd given up on her returning.

He picked up as much as he could get in the bag, and only realized one of Noah's drawings was on an envelope when a piece of paper fluttered to the floor. A lined white sheet, folded in three.

It was a letter. In Amy's handwriting.

He should have put it away, back in the tote, and not given it another thought. It wasn't his business, and he had no right to intrude. He stared at it for a moment longer, and then he started reading.

IT WAS JUST past six and Noah was eating the apple and cheese Becca had given him. She wasn't hungry. But he needed her to be normal, to be positive and to not think about what tomorrow would bring.

Thank goodness she'd remembered to bring in the flashlight from the trunk of her car, along with the rest of the road safety kit, which not only had a blanket but a rolled-up sleeping bag that Noah was excited about.

Tonight would work out fine, even though he was missing out on a bowl of chicken and dumplings. But by tomorrow, he'd have everything a little boy would want and need. A warm bath, a fully stocked kitchen. Toys and horses and cows and ATVs and love and…

She had to stop. Focus on the moment. She watched him take a bite of his apple. He looked so small sitting in her grandfather's broken recliner.

The sound of an engine drew her to the window. Ryder parked close to the house, and behind him, was another truck. Wiley's?

At least this time she wasn't sobbing, so that was something. She'd thought she wouldn't see him until tomorrow. Maybe he'd brought the cooler? Some dinner for Noah?

He knocked on the door, and Noah put his food on the chair before he ran to answer it, but Becca got there first, a bit breathless. "Ryder?"

He looked solemn but not upset. Although something felt off about him. God, she hoped nothing had happened to Gail.

"We need to talk for a minute. In private. Wiley's going to take Noah to the ranch. Mom wants to give him a hot dinner."

"All right," Becca said slowly, "but not for too long…"

Noah started jumping up and down. "On the ATV?"

Wiley stepped around Ryder and grabbed the boy's jacket and his hat. "Nope. We're going by truck. You like the truck." He helped him into his jacket and stuck the hat on his head. "Wave bye to Mommy."

Noah turned and gave her a half-hearted wave, all too ready to run out the door before anything could stand in his way. Becca guessed he wasn't as excited about his "'venture" as she'd thought.

The door closed behind Wiley, and Ryder moved closer. Close enough that she could see the look in his eyes and it made the hair on the back of her neck rise. "Is there something you forgot to tell me?" he asked. The cold of his voice made her blanch.

"What are you talking about?" She swallowed. He knew. Somehow he knew. How? How much?

"Oh, really? Nothing at all? Nothing you've been holding back?"

"Ryder, you're scaring me."

"Gee, sorry. Guess when I discovered you've been lying to me and my family for the last four years, I might have gotten a little upset."

"Now wait," she said, holding up a hand.

"Wait? What for? Until you can take Noah away and never tell us that he's Amy's child? That he's my mother's *grandson*?"

Every muscle in her body clenched and the urge to run was so strong it was hard to ignore. "You don't understand. There's more to it than you know. I had to make sure before I told you. That your family was—that you deserved him."

He opened his mouth, but nothing came out. His fists clenched along with his jaw. He'd read the letter. That was all that made sense, but how? Had she left it behind? No. That wasn't possible. Only Noah's toys had…

"You had no right to read that. It was personal. To me."

"*I* had no right."

She closed her eyes, but only for a second. "I was going to tell you. Tomorrow. But if you read the letter, you know why I hadn't told you before. Amy told me things that weren't true."

"But you had to know they were lies. You practically lived at our house. We were nothing but kind to you. But what did you do? Lied. Lied about everything. You knew that Amy was in trouble, and you kept your mouth shut. Did you hope she'd stay with her abuser so you wouldn't have to fight her over Noah? Was that your plan all along?"

"Plan? You think I planned for Amy to get pregnant and plead with me not to tell anyone? To put her child into my arms and beg me to keep him and that she'd get better soon? But she never did get better, did she? I couldn't have talked to you, because she swore you and your father were monsters. Was I just supposed to think she was kidding?"

"Stop blaming Amy! Hasn't she paid enough of a price?"

Becca flinched.

"What about before the drugs, huh? You watched her fall into a depression over her future, and what did you do about it? You could have called your grandparents, or even your mother. Asked any of them to find out the truth about the family. But evidently they didn't trust you either."

Becca blinked. "What do you mean they didn't trust me?"

Ryder stayed silent, his expression now eerily devoid of emotion, as if he'd used up all his energy.

"I tried to protect Noah. That's all I've ever done." Becca didn't give one damn about Ryder. He was dead wrong, and he was wrong about her mother, wrong about everything. "After Amy hooked up with Derek, there was no getting through to her. I could have left Noah with social services, would that have been better? I took him in from day one. Spent everything I had taking care of him. Amy kept promising she'd want him back as soon as she got better. And I never gave up on her."

All Ryder did was shake his head. She could tell he hadn't listened to a word she'd said. He had his own version, where Amy wasn't to blame for anything. And neither was he, and neither was his perfect family. Just Becca. She was the one who'd done everything wrong.

And now he had Noah.

"I swear to God I was going to tell you everything tomorrow. I couldn't let Gail hurt like that. I knew you deserved to know the truth. I planned on moving back to Blackfoot Falls. To keep Noah close to all of us."

Ryder laughed. "Pretty damn convenient timing, I'd say." He turned to the door but stopped. "And by the way, this house," he said, his voice flat, "your mother sold it to me two years ago. I expect you to be out of here by morning."

He didn't wait for a response. He just threw the door open, then stormed out to his truck.

She ran after him, desperate, panicked. "Where did you take Noah? He's going to be frightened. I'm the only mother he's ever known. Don't punish him like this."

Opening the driver's door, Ryder paused. "You think I'd give you the chance to disappear with him?"

"I wouldn't do that—"

He'd already climbed in and slammed the door. The truck backed up with a squeal, and then Ryder sped away, taking her whole world with him.

She fell to her knees, no longer able to bear the agony. Noah. Wiley had taken Noah. Ryder had taken everything. Shaking uncontrollably, she still managed to pull out her cell phone to call Gail. Becca would explain. Gail needed to understand because Ryder didn't. He didn't understand that she'd done nothing but love Noah. That she couldn't live without him. That she was his mother in every way but blood. And now he'd be terrified and wonder why she'd abandoned him.

The line was busy.

She tried one more time and got another busy signal. Then she rested back on her legs, her heart dissolving in her chest, and dialed her mother's number. Unbelievably, Katie answered.

"Becca! It's so wonderful to hear from you. We just got back from the Environmental Agency up north. Just in time, too. They were snowed under a couple hours after we left."

"Mom."

"Seriously, it was crazy, but we got so much done. Anyway, Scott's still unloading and I've got to check the fridge, see if anything—"

"Mom! Stop!"

"Honey, what's wrong?"

"Did you sell Grams's house?"

"Of course I did."

"When?"

"Just after I settled Grams's will. I'm sure I told you."

"No, you didn't."

"Well, it didn't matter all that much. Ryder Mitchell gave us a good price and agreed to let me leave some of our things. Grams wanted some of the proceeds set aside in a trust for you, which I did, but that won't be available until you turn twenty-five."

Becca thought she'd cried all the tears she had. But there were still more left. Although, she really shouldn't be surprised Katie had forgotten… "I turned twenty-five six months ago."

Katie sighed. "I'm so sorry, honey. I know, I get so caught up in my own life sometimes."

Sometimes? "I'll talk to you later, Mom. I have to go." Becca hung up. A trust. She had no idea how much it was for, but whatever it was, she sure could have used it months ago. Maybe there would've been enough for her to get Amy into a good rehab. And to have gotten Noah new clothes and for him to see the dentist, maybe even get him out of the neighborhood.

But what did it matter now?

Everyone Becca had ever believed in had let her down. And, she supposed, she'd let them down, too.

God, she'd messed up everything. Even the life of the boy she loved more than life itself.

Chapter Twenty

Ryder arrived home and just sat in his truck for a few minutes, heavy with exhaustion and feeling utterly betrayed. Becca had betrayed all of them. Had she really thought he'd believe that she'd planned to tell them everything tomorrow? He'd bet the reason she'd moved out of the house was so she could sneak away. Leave his mother to wonder what she'd done wrong, when all she'd done was treat Becca and Noah like family.

He shook it off and went around the back, through the mudroom to the kitchen, where his mom was checking on something in the oven.

At the sound of his boots, she made a quick turn. "Ryder? What's wrong? I thought you were taking dinner to Becca and Noah?"

He couldn't just tell her he'd taken Noah and that Wiley had him in the bunkhouse for now, even though it was for the boy's own good. The letter was burning a hole in his pocket and he couldn't wait to pull it out. "You should sit down."

Looking worried, she turned off the oven before using her cane to help her to the table. She sat, trembling. He was sorry about that, but once she knew the truth and had her grandson, that would make up for so much. A part of Amy, living right here, without the threat of Becca taking him away.

He unfolded the letter and set it down on the table. "This won't be easy, but once you understand what's going on, we'll talk. I'll be right here."

She lifted the paper. Her brow furrowed deeper, and her face paled. He couldn't watch. Instead, he poured himself a cup of coffee, his stomach complaining before he took the first sip, then stared out the window. He knew Wiley was keeping Noah busy; he just hoped the kid wasn't scared.

He'd talk it over with his mother. Decide what to tell Noah. Nothing too much for a four-year-old. The real story wouldn't come out until he was old enough to understand.

"Ryder, where did this letter come from?"

"That's Amy's handwriting."

"That's not what I asked."

His mother looked appropriately stunned, although she sounded awfully calm. He carried his cup to the table, but he couldn't sit. He didn't like how she was looking at him. "It's all there in black and white. It fell out of Becca's bag. I didn't mean to read it, but when I saw it was written by Amy—"

"You read this, and then you left the house like a man on fire. What happened?"

"What happened is that Becca lied to us. From the very beginning."

She nodded, her expression troubled, confused. "She's been through a great deal with Amy and Noah."

Ryder studied her closely. He hoped she wasn't having another stroke. "But she could have called. Gotten Amy out of there, before that scum got a hold of her."

"I have some thoughts about that, but I can't help but

wonder why you believe Becca wouldn't have told us everything in her own time."

"What, when Noah was in college? You sure do have a lot of faith in the woman who's been keeping your grandson from you. I'm sorry if I can't share that confidence."

"Can't or won't? You know Becca didn't want to go to LA in the first place. At least now I understand why she felt it so necessary to go and use all her savings to get them there."

Gail looked back at the letter with her shoulders hunched and pain in every line in her face. "It hurts my heart to know that Amy would say those things about you and your father just so she could get away. I thought we had a better relationship. I truly did."

It only hit him then that he should never have shown his mother the letter. What an idiot he was. So caught up in his disappointment, he hadn't taken a minute to consider how she'd feel about Amy's lies.

He slid into the seat across from her. "Becca knew us. She'd practically lived here. She had to know Amy was manipulating her."

"Oh, Ryder." His mom shook her head. "You might've had feelings for Becca, but I don't think you truly know her. When her grandmother offered to send money after they left for California, Becca refused, even though she had to be struggling. She wanted to stand on her own two feet. Of course, she had more than herself to worry about. Even those early years, I doubt Amy was taking her work responsibilities too seriously. And then after the baby, Becca had to support both of them. She was twenty-one when Noah was born. That was a heavy load to carry."

Ryder bowed his head, hating how much he'd hurt his mom.

"Why she had to be so vicious, though, I don't… Amy,

not Becca," Gail clarified. "To say such things about her father. He worked so hard to make this ranch a success for all of us. He'd never hurt a fly. And you, heavens, no. You were always such a good brother." She sighed, wiping a tear. "I can't help but think that horrible lie played a part in Amy's addiction. The guilt must've eaten at her, and what better way to forget but to lose herself in drugs?

"Oh, that poor, misguided girl. She could have come home. Even after she'd said all that, none of us would have turned her away."

Christ, Ryder wanted to go back in time, to never have given her that damn letter. To have come up with some other reason for all this trouble with Becca. "If I hadn't seen the letter with my own eyes, I wouldn't have believed it myself. I'm really sorry I didn't think first. You should never have had to know all that."

"I wouldn't like you carrying that burden on your own. I'm just sorry it happened."

"I'm still not convinced that Becca couldn't have found a way to get through to Amy."

"Didn't you tell me she tried to get Amy into rehab or a women's shelter?"

Ryder nodded, feeling the prick of his own guilt.

"I'm sure Becca did her best. You know, she could have just gotten out of there. Gone somewhere else. But she stayed, first for Amy, then for Noah. She gave up her life for them, don't you see? Gave up her dreams. I believe that, no matter what, Becca put Noah's well-being first. Including bringing him out here to make sure Amy wasn't lying again."

He sat back in his chair, closed his eyes for a moment, wanting to scrub his thoughts clean, to not feel so torn up. He remembered Becca saying she hadn't dated in five years. At twenty-one, would he have taken on someone else's kid? He'd been all about getting his degree, getting Leanne and expanding the ranch. He could barely see anything aside from his goals, and he'd have dared anyone to try to impede him.

The early twenties were a time for exploring what you wanted, going full out reaching for your dreams, finding out what you were made of.

He guessed Becca had learned that last part the hard way. She'd stayed loyal to Amy, to Noah. She'd taken on an enormous responsibility that wasn't hers to assume in the first place. His anger had lot more to do with himself than with Becca. She'd been a far better person than him.

What he needed to do was think this through. Rationally. Before he botched up everything. Just like he had his marriage.

"Noah's here," he said, the confession harder than he'd imagined.

"Where?"

"In the bunkhouse. With Wiley."

"You took him away from Becca?"

He'd never seen condemnation in his mom's eyes, at least not before today. "She could've left tonight. Disappeared with him. I couldn't take that chance."

"You go get him right now." She was trembling again, but he could see it was from anger.

In fact, she looked stronger than she had in a long time. Stronger than all those times he'd left her alone while he'd taken off on *business*. The thought cut right through him.

Ryder stood, feeling like a stupid five-year-old, yet still fighting the urge to blame it all on everyone but himself. Clear thoughts. Hold the judgment. Even on himself. He needed to take one step at a time.

On his way to the bunkhouse, the only thing he was

pretty damn sure of was that whatever feelings Becca might have ever had for him were gone forever.

BECCA HAD SLEPT in fits and starts, and every time she woke up, it was from a nightmare that she'd lost Noah. But the reality was so much worse. She wished she'd had something more than water to drink. Even the apple juice she'd brought for Noah had made her ill.

What she hadn't expected was how devastated she felt over Ryder's reaction. She hadn't even realized that what she'd been feeling for him was love. Considering the blow he'd been dealt over Amy's death, he'd come around and been strong and steady, a shoulder to lean on, just as she'd imagined him in her teenage fantasies. But that's all they were, that's what she'd fallen for…the fantasies. She knew he was in shock and grieving, and she could forgive him some of his behavior but…

Oh, it was no use thinking about him. Again.

It was barely past dawn. Her eyes burned, she was chilled to the bone despite the heat of the stove and packing had been like digging her own grave. All she really had left was her job. And a three-day ultimatum from her boss, which gave her little time to somehow convince Gail to agree to visitation. It wouldn't be often, sadly, but she'd get back even if she had to use every penny of her apparent trust fund to buy a new car.

It was only sixteen hours to Blackfoot Falls.

Surely Gail would be reasonable, even if she agreed with Ryder. Gail was a mother first—she'd understand that cutting Becca off from Noah would hurt him.

Her eyes welled again, and she ruthlessly brushed the tears away. What good was crying? All it did was make it more difficult to see, to think. Right now, she needed every tool in her arsenal. She'd inevitably see Ryder, and she couldn't stand it if she fell apart in front of him again. How he hated her now was another huge bruise to her heart. She knew she should hate him, too. But she didn't.

Well, that just proved she was delusional. Or so naive she was a danger to humanity, not to mention herself.

All she needed to do was stay strong. Keep it together. Ask nicely to speak to Gail alone. And if Ryder didn't allow that, which was likely, she'd block him out, like the sirens and the gunfire in her neighborhood. She'd just speak to Gail's heart. Explain to her that she never would have stayed silent about Noah. She couldn't have, even though the thought had more than just crossed her mind.

There was no point in lying about anything. Her only hope was with the truth. She'd grovel, she'd beg. Whatever was necessary. But she wasn't leaving without knowing she'd see Noah again.

She just wished she didn't have to see Ryder, too.

If only he'd given her a chance. If only he'd listened to her. That he hadn't, she couldn't forgive.

No. She shouldn't think about him. Not in that way. He had his reasons for being angry. She'd been angry herself and probably made things worse.

Now it was time to load her car and make that short drive to the Sundowner.

Her lightweight coat didn't block the morning cold. The temperature had dropped, just in time for her to try to start her lousy engine. She hoped she wouldn't have to walk to the ranch.

When she looked back at her grandparents' house, a wave of nostalgic sadness swept over her. It would always be their house in her mind. And her heart.

Her thoughts stopped the moment she heard the unique purr of Ryder's truck coming up behind her.

She left the last bag on the ground as she straightened

her shoulders. If he wanted to personally kick her out, that was fine. Of course he'd see she was a wreck, but he hadn't broken her.

He parked, and when he stepped out of the truck wearing a long Sherpa-lined coat, gloves and his hat, she figured she could probably hate him after all.

"I'm leaving in a minute," she said. "Don't worry. I haven't stolen anything. I'm just taking the things my mom left for me."

"That's not why I'm here." He sounded calm, but he'd played that card before, and it hadn't turned out well for her.

"Why, then?"

"To apologize. Again," he said and her heart fluttered. "And to offer you a job."

"What, you'll pay me to stay away from Noah? No, thanks."

Ryder shook his head and sighed. "I'd appreciate it if you'd hear me out, even though you'd probably rather slap me."

"No probably about it," she muttered, folding her arms across her chest. She was glad he looked terrible. Like he hadn't slept either. He should. "Go on."

"I said things I shouldn't have, things I didn't even mean." He removed his hat and stared at it in his hands. "I don't want you to go, Becca. Nobody wants you to."

"Gail isn't angry with me?"

"Not even a little. The only person who has reason to be angry is you."

God, please, no more tears. She blinked furiously. "Tell me about this job."

He looked up, his face ashen, and he really did look awful, but a glint of hope entered his eyes. "Well, my mom's going to need help. I'd like you to stay and help take care of Noah. I'll pay you anything you want."

Stunned, with her heart racing, she wanted to leap at the chance, but this didn't solve the whole problem. She should hate the sight of Ryder, but her feelings for him hadn't gone away. *All fantasies*, she reminded herself.

"Look, you know Noah's a handful, and my mother isn't getting any younger."

Could she really see Ryder almost every day? Watch him date other women, marry one someday? She swallowed. Of course she could, if it meant being close to Noah.

His face fell. Any stoicism he'd been holding vanished with his look of shame. "I'm sorry, Becca. I was a hotheaded fool last night. I said cruel things, and taking Noah away like that? I don't think I'll ever outlive the shame I feel."

"I made my share of mistakes, too."

"Hey," he said, stepping closer. "No. I was a goddamn coward. I don't even really want to hire you, but that's the only thing I could come up with to keep you here. What I really want is your forgiveness. I've known you since you were a girl. A sweet, responsible, levelheaded kid. You haven't changed. You've been loyal to the end. I'm the one who's failed everyone I've cared about..."

Becca swallowed. She'd known him, too. He was wrong. That was the only reason she could forgive him. And yet...

He turned his head to face the wind, then after a moment, he turned to her again, looking surprised that she'd moved a step closer.

"I knew you, too, your family," Becca said. "I never should have believed Amy's lies. I don't know why I did. I felt guilty that I'd missed the clues—"

"Hey." He touched her arm, briefly, letting his fingers trail away. "Don't. Amy was your friend. You had no reason to doubt her."

"How's Noah?"

"Asking for you."

She bit her lip.

"Last night he wanted to sleep in the bunkhouse with the rest of the cowboys. 'Course about three this morning, Wiley brought him to my bedroom door. Noah had decided he wasn't so happy in the bunkhouse."

She nodded, held back a smile.

"I know I have no right to say this or think you'll ever look at me again without feeling disgust, but do you think you could give me another chance? Give us a chance to get to know each other better? If I'd truly understood you, I'd never have dreamed you had anything but the best intentions. I'd like to make up for that. But I also understand that giving me another chance might be too much to ask."

She put out her hand and he held it in his. She felt his pulse quicken, or maybe it was hers.

"I want to be real clear," Ryder said. "Yes, I want you here for Noah's sake, and also for my mom. But I want you here for me, too, Becca. I think we could really have something." He took a shaky breath. "But if you can't stay because of me, then I'll step aside. Noah needs his mother."

"What?" Her voice dropped to a whisper. "What did you say?"

"You are his mother, Becca." He wiped a tear off her cheek. "A damn good one. No question about that."

She looked at their hands, how they seemed to fit together so perfectly. Then she looked into his earnest gaze.

"I didn't realize I'd become such a hothead, and I need to work on that. Frankly, I could learn a lot from you.

Please give me a shot at becoming the kind of man who deserves you."

More tears stung her eyes. "I have a question for you. Do you think you'll ever be able to trust me again?"

"Oh, honey, I think in my heart I always trusted you. It was me. I didn't want to think I'd failed. Mom. Amy. You." He kissed her fingertips. "I promise I'll focus on you and Noah and not take so many business trips. Hell, we have enough to do here, we don't need a bigger ranch anyway."

Becca smiled. She knew it would take time. For them to grieve, to rebuild. She was still shaky, and she had a lot to lose if things didn't work out.

But if they did, it would mean everything. A family, Noah, Ryder, Gail. A safe home and a future that held everything good. And just maybe there was more to those fantasies, after all.

Looking into Ryder's pleading eyes, she took one more step. A huge one.

"Yes," she said. "Yes. I'd like us to try." He kissed her palm, then picked her up and kissed her lips.

"I promise to never make you regret this," he whispered and hugged and kissed her until she couldn't breathe.

Epilogue

Two Christmases later...

"Noah. No running. And remember your manners."

"Okay, Mommy," he said, running straight through the front door of Grandma's house to the giant tree and the presents that surrounded it.

Becca sighed, but Ryder just chuckled. "You'd think he didn't get presents last night and this morning."

"It's not spoiling him if they're just stocking stuffers."

"Right," he said, but she knew he was spoiling the stuffing out of her. He'd given her a beautiful new home, filled with every gadget she'd ever dreamed of and more, and even better, a wedding beyond her imagination. Not that it had been all that fancy, but it had been *their* wedding.

Now it was her turn to give Ryder his gift. She slowed him down with a hand on his arm. "I have something to tell you."

He stopped, looked at her with such love it made her heart swell. "What's that?"

She took his hand in hers and pulled it gently toward her tummy. "Can you guess what it is?"

His jaw dropped as his gaze moved from her face to her stomach to her face. "Really?"

"Yep."

"When?"

"Seven months."

He pulled her into his arms and hugged her too tight, then not tight enough. "You feeling all right?"

"Nothing terrible so far, just a little queasy sometimes."

"What are we doing standing out in the cold? You need some hot tea and crackers."

She laughed. "Oh, no. I'm having hot cocoa."

He nodded but herded her in as if she were a stray calf. Noah was already opening his presents. Now that he was six, he'd expanded his focus to dinosaurs, fire trucks and superheroes. Naturally, Gail had indulged him in every category.

Not that Becca and Ryder hadn't. Even though they'd only been in their new home just up the hill for six months, they'd gone all out for Christmas as well.

Gail's walker and cane hadn't been used in ages, and now that Wiley was a full-time fixture in her life, she'd been happier than Ryder had seen her in years.

Amy's memory was kept alive in pictures and many, many stories of good times through her childhood. And like last year, there was a very special ornament on the tree, one with her picture on it.

Once Ryder had Becca settled on the couch, Gail walked over with two cups of cocoa that she set on the coffee table. Then she sat next to Becca and looked right at her tummy. "You told him?"

"What?" Becca asked, her surprise as genuine as Ryder's.

"You told her first?" Ryder asked.

"Of course she didn't," Gail said. "I just knew."

Ryder didn't understand, and from the look of it, neither did Becca. But that was okay. The news was so good, nothing in the world could matter more.

* * * * *

MILLS & BOON

Coming next month

MISS WHITE AND THE SEVENTH HEIR
Jennifer Faye

Of all the bedrooms, why did she have to pick that one?

Trey frowned as he struggled to get all five suitcases up the stairs. The woman really needed to learn how to pack lighter.

At the top of the steps, he paused. It was a good thing he exercised daily. He rolled the cases back down the hallway to the very familiar bedroom. The door was still ajar.

"Sage, it's just me." He would have knocked but his hands were full trying to keep a hold on all of the luggage.

There was no response. Maybe she'd decided to explore the rest of the house. Or perhaps she was standing out on the balcony. It was one of his favorite spots to clear his head.

But two steps into the room, he stopped.

There was Sage stretched across his bed. Her long dark hair was splayed across the comforter. He knew he shouldn't stare, but he couldn't help himself. She was so beautiful. And the look on her face as she was sleeping was one of utter peace. It was a look he'd never noticed during her wakeful hours. If you knew her, you could see something was always weighing on her mind. And he'd hazard a guess that it went much deeper than the trouble with the magazine.

Though he hated to admit it, he was impressed with the new format that she'd rolled out for the magazine. But he wasn't ready to back down on his campaign to close the magazine's doors. None of it changed the fact that to hurt his father in the same manner that he'd hurt him, the magazine had to go. It had been his objective for so many years. He never thought he'd be in a position to make it happen—but now as the new CEO of QTR International, he was in the perfect position to make his father understand in some small way the pain his absence had inflicted on him.

Trey's thoughts returned to the gorgeous woman lying on his bed sound asleep. She was the innocent party—the bystander that would get hurt—and he had no idea how to protect her. The only thing he did know was that the longer he kept up this pretense of being her assistant instead of the heir to the QTR empire—the worse it was going to be when the truth finally won out—and it would. The truth always came to light—sometimes at the most inopportune times.

Continue reading
MISS WHITE AND THE SEVENTH HEIR
Jennifer Faye

Available next month
www.millsandboon.co.uk

LET'S TALK *Romance*

For exclusive extracts, competitions and special offers, find us online:

- facebook.com/millsandboon
- @millsandboonuk
- @millsandboon

Or get in touch on 0844 844 1351*

For all the latest titles coming soon, visit millsandboon.co.uk/nextmonth

*Calls cost 7p per minute plus your phone company's price per minute access ch